When I looked at these other girls for the first time . . .

I realized that no one was happy to be here. Not one of us had come willingly. . . .

Yesterday, Star talked about times in her life when it felt like it was raining pain. I knew what she meant. Our worlds were very different, but similar clouds had come rolling in and we were under an identical downpour of anger and hate drenching us in our parents' madness. I guess we were all just people who had been caught in the same flood and had been pulled onto the same raft, now tossing and turning, all of us looking desperately for an end to the storm. . . .

JADE

V.C. Andrews® Books

The Dollanganger Family Series:
Flowers in the Attic
Petals on the Wind
If There Be Thorns
Seeds of Yesterday
Garden of Shadows

The Casteel Family Series:
Heaven
Dark Angel
Fallen Hearts
Gates of Paradise
Web of Dreams

The Cutler Family Series:
Dawn
Secrets of the Morning
Twilight's Child
Midnight Whispers
Darkest Hour

The Landry Family Series:
Ruby
Pearl in the Mist
All that Glitters
Hidden Jewel
Tarnished Gold

The Logan Family Series:
Melody
Heart Song
Unfinished Symphony
Music in the Night
Olivia

The Orphans Miniseries:
Butterfly
Crystal
Brooke
Raven
Runaways

My Sweet Audrina (does not belong to a series)

The Wildflowers Miniseries:
Misty
Star
Jade

Published by POCKET BOOKS

V.C. ANDREWS®

JADE

POCKET BOOKS
New York London Toronto Sydney Tokyo Singapore

Following the death of Virginia Andrews, the Andrews family worked with a carefully selected writer to organize and complete Virginia Andrews' stories and to create additional novels, of which this is one, inspired by her storytelling genius.

This book is a work of fiction. Names, characters, places and incidents are products of the author's imagination or are used fictitiously. Any resemblance to actual events or locales or persons, living or dead, is entirely coincidental.

An *Original* Publication of POCKET BOOKS

POCKET BOOKS, a division of Simon & Schuster Inc.
1230 Avenue of the Americas, New York, NY 10020

ISBN: 0-671-02802-2

First Pocket Books paperback printing September 1999

10 9 8 7 6 5 4 3 2 1

Cover illustration by Lisa Falkenstern
Cover design by Tony Greco

Printed in the U.S.A.

JADE

Prologue

Even though I had been in Dr. Marlowe's office many times, for some reason I couldn't recall the miniature grandfather clock in the center of the bottom wall shelf to the left of her desk. It was encased in dark cherry wood and had a face of Roman numerals. It didn't bong or clang. It played no music on the hour, but the small pendulum swung back and forth with a determined little effort that caught my eye and held me mesmerized for a few moments while everyone waited for me to begin.

The beat of my heart seemed synchronized with the movement of the miniature clock's pendulum, and I thought, why can't we think of our hearts as being little clocks inside us, keeping our time. Even before we are born, our parents' magical hands of love wind them up. Maybe the lengths of our lives are in direct proportion to how much our parents wanted us. Maybe some behavioral scientist should do a study of unwanted children to see how long they live and compare their lives with the lives of children from perfect little families. None of us in this room would probably be happy with those results.

I could feel the other girls' eyes on me and just knew what each of them must be thinking. What was I doing here? I looked like I came from one of those perfect little families. How horrible could my story be? Why did I need the services of a psychiatrist?

I could understand why they would have these questions. No matter what had happened between my mother and father and to me afterward, I always held myself together, poised, with a regal air of confidence. I guess I get that from my mother, although my father is far from being an insecure person. It's just that my mother will never let anyone know she is at a disadvantage. Even if she loses an argument, she does it in such a way that the winner isn't sure he or she has won. Her eyes don't fill with surrender. Her shoulders never sag; she never lowers her head in defeat.

Mother gets angry, but Mother doesn't lose control. Control is in fact the essence of who she is. My father wants me to believe that it is exactly her obsession with being in control that has led them to what he calls their marital apocalypse.

I suppose he's right in his characterization of it. It is the end of one world, a world I was innocent enough to believe would go on until their clocks ran out. I used to think they were so much in love, that when one's pendulum stopped, the other's would soon follow.

Of course, I told myself that wouldn't be until many, many years into the future when even I was entering old age. Our world was so protected, I believed I lived in a grand bubble that kept out fatal illness, serious accidents, crime and unhappiness. I went from a luxurious Beverly Hills home to plush limousines to private schools with sparkling clean hallways and new desks. I came out of one womb to be placed safely into another, never to be too cold or too hot.

In the world in which I grew up, being uncomfortable was intolerable, a betrayal of promises. Shoes had to fit perfectly, socks had to be soft, no clothes could chafe our skin. Our meals had to be properly cooked and sufficiently warm, our bathwater just the right temperature. Our beds smelled fresh or were deliciously scented. We fell asleep on clouds of silk and refused to admit nightmares into our houses of dreams. If one slipped under my door when I was a little girl, my father or mother was there instantly at the sound of my cry to step on it as they would some wicked little insect that dared show itself on our imported Italian marble floors.

I didn't think of myself as being exceptionally lucky or even fortunate. I was born into a life of luxury and it was there for me to discover and very quickly to expect. I had no deep philosophical explanation as to why I had so much and people I saw outside my limousine windows had so much less. Some great power had decided it would be this way and this was the way it was. That's all.

Of course, as I grew older and my mother talked about the things she had accomplished in her life and my father did the same, I understood that they had earned or won what we had and we therefore deserved it.

"Never be ashamed for having more than someone else," my mother once told me. More often than not when she made these pronouncements, she sounded like a lecturer. "Those with less are not ashamed of wanting more and especially wanting what you have. Envy always gives birth to resentment. Be careful to whom you give your trust. More than likely they have eyes greener than yours behind their dark glasses and artificial smiles," she warned.

How wise I thought she was. How wise I thought they both were.

Now here I sat after that magic bubble had burst and people who were really little more than strangers to me wanted me to give them my trust. The four of us were participating in what our therapist called group therapy, telling about ourselves, our most intimate selves in the hopes that we would somehow help each other understand and accept all that had happened to us. The more truthful we were about our intimate selves, the better the chances for success. That did take a great deal of trust.

From the way Dr. Marlowe talked, winning our

trust was more important to her than the money she received for trying to help us to readjust.

I love that term, readjust. It makes it seem as if we are all some broken mechanical thing that our psychiatrist will repair with a turn of a screw here, a bolt replaced there, and lots of new oil and grease squeezed into places that grind and squeak.

When I looked at these other girls for the first time, I realized that no one was happy to be here. Not one of us had come here willingly. Oh, I don't mean we were dragged here kicking and screaming, although Star made it sound as if it was almost that way for her. It's for sure we would each like to be someplace else. Cathy, whom we nicknamed Cat, hadn't even told her story yet, but one look at her face and I knew she dreaded being here the most. Maybe she dreaded being anywhere. Misty looked the least uncomfortable, but still stirred and fidgeted about like someone sitting on an ant hill, her eyes shifting nervously from one of us to the other.

Yesterday, Star talked about times in her life when it felt like it was raining pain. Even though she came from a much different world, I knew what she meant. Our worlds were very different, but similar clouds had come rolling in and we were under an identical downpour of anger and hate drenching us in our parents' madness. I guess we were all just people who had been caught in the same flood and had been pulled onto the same raft, now tossing and turning, all of us looking desperately for an end to the storm.

However, now that I was here and it was my turn to

talk about my life, I felt like I had been shoved into the center of this circle of eyes and ears. For two days I had been on the outside looking in, listening first to Misty and then to Star. I was able to maintain distance between myself and the others and to stay aloof like my mother, maybe I had inherited her desire for control. Today was my day and suddenly, I felt naked, conscious of every blemish, like some specimen under glass in our science class lab. Tears are more private than smiles, I thought. Why should I share any of them with these girls?

Look at them: Misty sitting there with her silly little grin and her tee shirt proclaiming *Boycott Child Labor, End Teenage Pregnancy;* Star, a black girl who was ready to jump down my throat every time I opened my mouth; and Cathy, a mousy-faced girl, who looked terrified enough to swallow her own tongue every time she blurted a comment and we turned to her. These three were to be my new confidants, my adopted sisters of misfortune? Hardly.

I wondered about this session all night, and then when the limousine brought me to Dr. Marlowe's house this morning, I sat there gazing at the front door and asked myself what was I doing here? The question still lingered. I'm not telling these people intimate things about myself just because they come from broken families, too. They're worse than strangers. They're so far from my world, they're foreigners. They'll just think I'm some spoiled brat.

"I can't do this," I declared and shook my head

after a long moment of silence and expectation. "It's stupid."

"Oh, I see. It wasn't stupid for me, yesterday," Star said, turning those ebony eyes of hers into tiny hot coals, "but it's stupid for you today."

"I don't think it was stupid for me either," Misty said, wide-eyed. "I don't!" she emphasized when I gave her a look that said, "Spare me."

Cat kept her eyes down. I felt like crawling on the floor, turning over on my back and looking up at her and asking, "Do you think it's all right to talk about your pain? And when you do, do we have to all lie down on the floor like this and look up at you?"

"You sat here and listened and made your comments about my life with no trouble yesterday," Star muttered.

"This isn't supposed to be show me yours and I'll show you mine. I didn't say I was going to do this for sure. I don't owe you anything just because you did it," I declared.

"I didn't say you did. You think I'm dying to hear your story?"

"Good, so I won't tell you anything," I said and practically turned my back on her.

"Very often," Dr. Marlowe said softly after a heavy moment of silence, "we use anger as a way of avoiding unpleasant things. Actually, anger only prolongs the unpleasantness and that only makes it harder for us."

"Us?" I fired at her.

"I'm human therefore I'm not perfect, so I say we, us. I understand these things from my own experiences, which helps me help you," she said. "Don't forget, I've been in the center, too. I know it's difficult and painful, but it helps."

"I don't see how just talking about myself is going to help me." I looked at Misty. "Do feel any better about yourself since you talked?"

She shrugged.

"I don't know if I feel any better. It felt like I unloaded some weight, though. Yeah," she said tilting her head in thought, "maybe I do feel better. What about you, Star?"

Star turned away.

"She doesn't care about what you feel or don't feel. She's just trying to run away," she said, jerking her head back toward me.

"Excuse me?" I said. "Run away? From what?"

"This is a process," Dr. Marlowe interjected, raising her voice a little. "A process that must be built on trust. I've said this before. You've got to try, Jade. Surely you've heard some things during these past two days that have helped you look at your own situation a little better. If anything, at least you know you're not alone."

"Oh no?" I said. "Not alone?" I stared at Misty for a moment. "I liked one thing you said during your session. I liked your classifying us as orphans with parents. Believe me, Dr. Marlowe," I said, turning back to her, "We're alone."

"The OWP! Let's get some tee shirts made up!"

Misty exclaimed with a bounce that made her look like she was sitting on springs.

"Yeah, it could be a whole new club," Star said dryly. She looked at me. "Or a new street gang with a Beverly as our leader."

"A Beverly?"

I shook my head. This is impossible. I shouldn't have agreed to take part in it.

"Just forget this," I muttered.

"You see, it's hard to begin, right?" Misty asked.

"It's because my situation is a lot different from yours," I declared.

"Sure," she said with a smirk that twisted her little nose. "You're special. We're not."

"Look. You told about your father leaving you and your mother and moving in with a girlfriend, right?"

"So?"

I looked at Star.

"And you told about parents that have deserted you and now you and your brother live with your grandmother, right?"

"Like she said, so?"

"So my situation is a lot different. My parents fought over me like cats in heat and they're still fighting over me. Neither will ever give the other the satisfaction. You don't know what that's like. I feel . . . I'm being pulled apart, poked to death with questions from lawyers, psychologists and judges!"

I didn't mean to scream it, but it came out that way, and tears bubbled in my eyes, too, as my throat closed with the effort to keep them back. Who wanted to cry in front of them?

Star turned to look at me. Cat lifted her eyes slowly as if they were heavy steel balls and Misty nodded, her eyes brightening. They all looked suddenly interested.

I took a deep breath. How could I make them understand? I wasn't being a snob. I spoke again, slowly, my eyes on the floor, probably looking at the same tile Cat stared at most of the time.

"When I first learned about my parents getting a divorce, I didn't think much about myself and with whom I'd be living. I just assumed fathers left and you stayed with your mother. I was almost sixteen when this all began and suddenly I became a prize to win in a contest. The contest was going to be held in a courtroom and my mother and father were going to try to prove to a judge that the other was unfit to have custody of me." I looked up at Star. "Do you have any idea what that's like?"

"No," she said quietly. "I don't. You're right. My parents both ran away from having custody and responsibility, but that doesn't mean I don't want to know what it's like to have parents who want you," she added.

The sincerity in her eyes took me by surprise. I felt the blood that had risen into my neck and cheeks recede, and my heart slowed as I sat back. I glanced at Dr. Marlowe, who had raised her eyebrows.

When I first began seeing Dr. Marlowe, I wanted to hate her. I wanted her to fail from the get-go. I don't know why. Maybe I didn't want to admit that I needed her. Maybe I still didn't, but I couldn't get myself to dislike her. She always seemed so relaxed. She didn't force me to do or say anything. She waited until the gates opened a little more in my mind and I let memories and feelings flow out. She was like that now.

I still felt twisted and stretched like a rubber band, but the butterflies in my stomach seemed to settle. Maybe I could do this. Maybe I should, I thought. Sometimes, when you hear yourself say things, you confirm your own feelings, and it was true, I didn't have anybody else to talk to these days except my face in the mirror.

I looked out the window. It was a much nicer day than yesterday. We didn't even have our usual marine layer flowing in from the ocean this summer morning. When I woke, the sky was already clear and bright. Now, as I sat staring into the soft blue sky, I could see birds flittering from branch to branch on the trees outside Dr. Marlowe's Brentwood house. A squirrel hurried down the trunk, paused, looked our way and scurried into a bush. I wished I could do the same.

Our house and grounds were bigger than Dr. Marlowe's, but we were only a few miles down Sunset Boulevard in one of the most expensive sections of Beverly Hills, a gated community of custom homes owned by some of the richest people in the country, maybe even the world. Our neighbors were ambassadors and business moguls, even Arab royalty owned homes there. It was one of the most desirable places to live. My parents had bought and built there knowing it would be. No wonder I grew up feeling like I was living in a protective bubble.

However, it wasn't difficult to be comfortable with our surroundings here. Dr. Marlowe was good at making me feel like I was just visiting with her. I didn't feel I was in treatment of any kind, although I knew that's exactly what this was. I supposed . . . no, I hoped, somewhere deep down that it was more, that I was with someone who cared about me for other than professional reasons.

Dr. Marlowe had told us she and her sister were children of divorce. They had ended up living with their father. Even though her experiences were different, there had to be some similarities, something that helped her to sympathize. She was right about that. It helped me to talk to her.

Maybe telling us a little about herself was just her way of getting the trust she was after. Maybe it was all part of the technique. Maybe I didn't care.

Maybe I did.

"I'm like everyone here," I admitted. "I don't want to hate my parents."

"Good," Dr. Marlowe encouraged. I could hear and sense the others relax. "That's a good start, Jade." Her eyes were full of expectation.

"Once they were in love," I said. "They had to have been in love. I saw all the pictures. They held hands and took walks on beaches. They smiled up at the camera while they sat at dinner tables. They had pictures of each other smiling and waving from horses, from cars and from boats. They were kissing under the Eiffel Tower in Paris, in a gondola in Venice, and even on a Ferris wheel in some amusement park. No two people could be more in love, I used to think.

"Now, I think, no two people could hate each other more."

I paused, feeling my face harden again with frustration and confusion.

"And I'm supposed to care about living with one more than the other."

"Do you?" Misty asked.

"No," I answered honestly. "Most of the time, I don't want to live with either of them."

"Whose fault is that?" Dr. Marlowe threw out at me. She had asked me this before and I had turned away. Now, I looked at the others. They all seemed so interested in my answer, even Cat stared intently at me.

I looked from one to the other, at their desperate eyes searching my face.

"I don't know!" I screamed back at them all.

"Me neither," Misty said.

Star just shook her head. She didn't have the answer either.

I looked at Cat. The terror was back in her eyes.

"That's what we're here to find out, then," Dr. Marlowe said. "You've all come so far. Why not take a few more big steps to see where it leads? Isn't that worth the effort, Jade?"

I turned away, tears burning under my lids.

"Jade?"

"Yes," I said finally.

I looked up at her through my tears.

"Okay," I said. "I'll try."

And I stepped out of that precious bubble again where the rain was cold and the sun was hot and people willingly and often told each other lies.

1

"As long as I can remember, both my parents always worked even though we never needed money. My mother has told me and reminded me even more often lately that for six months after I was born, she remained home to raise and nurture me. She always makes it sound like those six months were the ultimate sacrifice in her life. She says my father would never even think of taking a leave of absence to care for me even though he is essentially self-employed and doesn't have to answer to anyone but himself. That, she tells me, is a big difference between them and why I shouldn't even consider living with him.

"Now she tells me that new studies in women's magazines argue that the mother doesn't have to be at home during her child's formative years as much as was previously thought.

"Have you read that, too, Dr. Marlowe?" I asked.

"I've read similar arguments and data, but I haven't come to any definitive conclusions myself," she replied. "There are good arguments and data on the other side, too."

"Yes, well, I think she's been telling me that because Daddy says I would have had less emotional problems if my mother would have given me more tender loving care. I know for a fact that's part of my father's motion for custody."

I turned to the girls who looked lost. I hadn't heard Cat's story yet, but I knew neither Star nor Misty were really thrown into the lion's den of divorce courts. They were in for a real education listening to me.

"My father and his attorney claim my mother was insensitive to my needs. He says she was too self-centered and that was why they only had me. As soon as he realized what a poor mother she was going to be, he decided not to have any more children."

Star grunted.

"In my case and especially Rodney's, we were lucky our momma didn't spend more time on our formative years," she said. "Otherwise, we might never have formed at all."

Dr. Marlowe surprised us with a small laugh.

I continued.

"Of course, my mother says she decided not to have any more children because she knew what a poor father my father was and would continue to be. She said he couldn't blame his failings as a parent on her career. She claims it doesn't interfere with her responsibilities toward me."

"So your mother still works?" Misty asked.

"Are you kidding? Of course."

"What does your mother do?" Misty asked.

"She's a sales manager for a big cosmetics company—if you want, I could probably get your mother some real discounts," I said, remembering how she described her mother's obsession with her looks.

"My mother never worries about discounts," she replied. "The more she spends, the more she can complain about the alimony being too little to provide her with the lifestyle she was accustomed to before the divorce," Misty declared with a dramatic air that brought a smile to my face.

"You probably don't realize it, but that's an important legal consideration," I told her.

"What is?"

"The wife and the child or children enjoying the lifestyle they enjoyed before the divorce. It's one of the things the judge will consider to determine support payments should my mother win custody. My mother wants to be considered fully independent, but her attorney wants her to sue for some alimony so my father still bears his burden of expenses for her well-being as well as mine."

I paused and looked at them.

"Are you all sufficiently fascinated yet? Does this compare to your favorite soap opera?"

Misty held her smile in check.

"What's your father do?" Star asked.

"My father is an architect. He's actually a very successful one who designed some of the buildings in Los Angeles and one of the big malls now being built. He has designed buildings outside of California, too, and even did one in Canada. My mother and her attorney have tried to make a big thing of his travel to point out that he would be away too much to provide proper parental care and supervision, especially for a young teenage girl.

"Daddy says my mother's grueling schedule is worse than his and she, too, often travels on behalf of her company, so she would be away too much to provide proper care and supervision. They have subpoenaed each other's travel receipts, business diaries and credit card records to support their arguments in court."

I thought for a moment and looked at Dr. Marlowe.

"I've been wondering what will happen if the judge believes they are both right. That would leave me with parents who are both incapable of being proper parents, right, Dr. Marlowe?"

"That situation has occurred, of course, but I doubt it will in your case, Jade."

"Really. That's a relief," I said. "Otherwise, I might have had to move in with Star and her granny."

"Like you could stand one day without maids and chauffeurs and such," Star shot back.

Misty laughed and Cat smiled.

"Maybe you're right," I said, "but I can tell you

this . . . I'm not giving anything up to make their lives easier for them. They raised me to expect a luxurious life and that's what they have to provide. Enjoy the lifestyle to which I have been accustomed, remember?"

Everyone stopped smiling. I sat back.

"You all know I'm a Beverly. Star called me that just a few minutes ago," I said, looking at Misty who had told us about her boyfriend classifying spoiled rich girls as Beverlys because they came from Beverly Hills. "I'm not ashamed of being rich. I don't think of myself as being spoiled. I think of myself as being . . . protected."

"Against what?" Star asked. "Certainly not unhappiness."

"There are degrees of unhappiness and different things that make you unhappy. I don't have to worry about buying anything or going anywhere I want."

"Big deal," Star said.

"It is to me and no matter how you act here, I know it is to you too," I said recalling my mother's advice about people who had less.

"You don't know anything," Star fired back.

"Oh, and you do?"

She folded her arms and sat up straighter, putting herself in a defensive posture.

"Do you have a big house?" she asked me.

"Bigger than this in fact," I answered, looking around the office, which was admittedly quite large. It had a desk and bookcases on one end and the sofas, chairs and tables on the other with large windows facing the back yard. "My father designed our house, of course. It's not a Tudor like this one. He thought there were just too many Tudors in Los Angeles.

"We have what's called a two-story Neoclassical. It has a full-height, semicircular entry porch with Ionic columns. It has two side porches and all the windows are rectangular with double-hung sashes, nine panes to each sash. It's very unique and always gets a lot of attention. Cars actually slow down when they come up to it and people gape even though there are many other magnificent homes in the community.

"What is this house, Dr. Marlowe, four thousand square feet?" I asked her.

"Something like that," she said.

"Mine is closer to eight. Does that give you an idea?" I asked Star.

"So you have a big house. Do you have your own car?" Star questioned.

"I will have this year. I haven't decided what I want yet. My mother suggested I ask for a Jag convertible after my father had suggested a Ford Taurus. Now my father is thinking maybe a Mustang. They're both dangling carrots. Until I do decide, I have a limousine available whenever I need to go anywhere."

"Great. Glad you explained all that," Star quipped. "So you have transportation. I'll bet you also have lots of clothes."

"My walk-in is almost a third as long as this office and full of the latest trends." I glanced at Misty. "I know from what you told me you have nice things, but the difference is I wear mine. This gray sleeveless sheath I'm wearing today is a Donna Karan," I pointed out.

"I don't have anything that expensive," Misty said. "My mother does."

"You poor thing," Star said. She turned back to me. "And you have a maid and gardeners and a cook to go with your expensive wardrobe, I bet," she said.

"Yes, I do as a matter-of-fact. The current maid's name is Rosina Tores. She's about twenty-five and from Venezuela, and my cook's name is Mrs. Caron. She's from France and was once a cordon bleu cook for a famous restaurant."

"Our maid is our cook," Misty said. "You have a separate cook? Wow."

"So you have a big home and cars and a maid and a fancy cook and I still say, big deal," Star declared. "Stop paying the maid and the cook and limousine driver and you'll see how fast they stop caring about you," she added. "And when you go home, you just have more room for your loneliness in your great big house. With all your money, you can't buy what I have."

"What's that, poverty?"

"No, a granny who gives me love and not because she's hired to do it," she said with glee. She looked like a little girl sticking a pin into someone else's beautiful balloon.

I looked at Dr. Marlowe. Her eyes were fixed so hard on me, I felt my face grow warm.

"I have grandparents," I said.

"You do?" Misty asked, the expression on her face

looking as though she anticipated all sorts of warm stories about family gatherings and holidays. I hated to disappoint her almost more than I hated disappointing myself. Wait until they heard about my last Christmas, I thought.

"Yes, they just live far away. My father's parents live back East. He has two brothers and a sister and they are all married and have children, too. My mother's parents live in Boca Raton, Florida. They're retired. My mother has one brother who works on Wall Street. He's not married."

"What do your grandparents say about the divorce?" Misty asked.

"Not much, at least to me. My father's parents have told him to work out his problems and my mother's have told her they are too old to deal with these kinds of crises now. They want to be left to their golf and bridge games."

"Do they ask you to visit them?" Star wanted to know.

"They have, but not lately," I confessed. "They all probably think I'm a big mess and they can't deal with it. I don't like visiting with them anyway," I added. "There's nothing for me to do and they all complain too much about their aches and pains and digestion.

"Besides," I realized aloud, "if I decided to visit my father's parents, my mother would want me to visit hers and spend equal time."

"They'd fight over that?" Misty asked, astounded.

"They fight over postage stamps. My house is like

a war zone these days. Sometimes, I feel like I'm risking my life just walking between them."

"You mean, they both still live there in the house together?" Cat asked astonished.

I had almost forgotten about her because she was so quiet. I certainly didn't expect she was following my every word so closely.

"Yes, they do. Of course, they don't share the same bedroom anymore, but they are both at home when they're here in Los Angeles."

"Why?" Misty asked, grimacing. "I mean, if they are in the middle of a bad divorce and all, why would they want to still be living together?"

"My mother let it slip that at first my father wanted to move out, but his lawyer explained to him that in general, if one parent has moved out of the home without the child by the time the trial has started, it will be more difficult for that parent to win custody of the child. She says that's the only reason he's still with us."

"Wow," Misty said. "Your father must really love you if he is willing to stay in an emotional fire zone just because of that."

"Her mother could move out, but didn't. Don't forget that," Star reminded her.

"They're not doing it for me," I said through clenched teeth. I didn't realize I was pressing my teeth together, something I'd caught myself doing more and more lately.

"Who are they doing it for?" Cat asked.

"Themselves. I told you. I'm a prize, a trophy, a

way of one getting it over on the other. Don't you listen?"

She shook her head.

They all still looked confused about all these legal maneuvers that occurred in a custody battle. I gazed at Dr. Marlowe, who wore a small smile on her lips.

I sighed deeply, lifting and dropping my shoulders.

"I guess in a sense this legal war and my status as a trophy is my story," I said and truly began.

"My parents didn't have me until almost six years after they had gotten married. I always had a suspicion that I was a mistake. My mother forgot to take her birth control pills or I was one of the small percentage of pregnancies that can't be prevented. I like to think they had some wild passionate time and threw all caution to the wind, that the both of them, normally well-adjusted, perfect and organized people, were impulsive and made love when either least expected it. And, as a result: *moi.*"

I held out my arms. Misty laughed. Star let her lips soften into something of a smile. Cat just continued to stare wide-eyed, as if it was incredible to even think of such a fantasy.

"When I was about nine, I used to sit on the floor in the living room and look through their vacation albums and actually envision love scenes. As I told you, they went to so many romantic places. To me they seemed to have lived in a movie. I could even hear the music."

Misty lowered her chin to her hand and stared at me, a dreamy haze in her eyes as I continued.

"There they were in the gondola in Venice listening to the music and the singing and then afterward, rushing up to their hotel room, laughing, my mother throwing herself into my father's arms, and as the moonlight poured through the window and someone sang in the street below, they made me."

"Right," Star said. "It probably happened in the backseat of some car."

"Maybe for you," I snapped at her. "My father and mother would never . . ."

"Why are you lying to yourself? Don't enough people lie to you as it is?" she asked, angrily.

I stared at her and then looked at Dr. Marlowe, who raised her eyebrows, which was something I noticed she always did when she thought a valuable thought had been dangled before me, or any of us, for that matter.

"I'm not lying to myself. It might have been that way once. Both of you talked about your parents loving each other once and doing and saying nice things. Why couldn't it have been the same for mine?" I asked, my voice sounding almost like I was pleading.

Star looked away. In my heart I knew that she wanted to dream the same sort of fantasies, but was afraid of them after what she had been through. I guess I didn't blame her. Maybe she was right.

"My mother got pregnant," I said dryly, "and she was about to be promoted at work. That I know for a fact because I've heard it too many times for anyone to have made it up. So that's why I think I was probably an accident."

"Why didn't they just have an abortion?" Star asked.

"Sometimes, I think they did," I said.

It was like I was looking in three separate mirrors and saw my face in each of theirs. How many times recently had each of them felt the same way, a burden, unwanted?

"They wanted me and didn't want me. Their lives were less complicated without me and yet, I guess, grandparents, friends, society, kept them thinking about having children, starting a family. My mother was thirty-two and hovering over her shoulder, she says, like the good and bad angels, was this biological clock, the hands pointing at her like two thick forefingers, warning her time was running out.

"Anyway, once she discovered she was pregnant, they had the first of their many, what should I call them?" I wondered aloud looking at Dr. Marlowe. "Post-nuptial agreements?"

"What's that?" Star asked quickly.

"Lots of people today sign pre-nuptial agreements before they get married. Some do it to protect their personal assets or to guarantee things they don't want to change won't change just because they get married." I paused and laughed.

"As you see, thanks to my parents, I'm practically a paralegal.

"Anyway, my parents didn't have a pre-nuptial, but after they got married, they agreed certain things would always continue.

"Namely, my mother could pursue her career and

my father would do what he could to ensure that happened. Nature, and shall we say unprotected sex, had thrown a new ingredient into their lives, a fetus they would name Jade. I threatened their wonderful status quo so they had to reassure each other, understand?" I asked Star. She didn't look like she understood. "Do you?"

"I feel like I'm a nail and you're a hammer. I'm not stupid," she quipped.

"Well, I just want you to appreciate my situation."

"Appreciate?"

Frustrated, I looked at Dr. Marlowe. Couldn't she see how much more difficult this was for me? These girls were so . . . unsophisticated.

"You were telling them about the post-nuptial," she said firmly, insisting I keep trying. I sighed and continued.

"Yes, the post-nuptial. So they sat down and wrote out what they expected of each other if I were to be permitted to be born," I said.

"What are you telling us?" Star asked, her eyebrows rising like question marks. "If they disagreed about it, they wouldn't have had you?"

"Let me assure you," I replied, "I have little doubt, especially after the last six months or so."

Star shook her head.

"I swear," she said, "Granny's right. Rich folks are not just different. They are another species."

"I don't know that it's just money that makes people different," Misty offered. She looked at Cat, who bit down on her lower lip so hard, I was afraid she would draw blood. "Jade already told us her mother didn't have to work, and both her parents having careers made for big problems, right?" Misty asked Dr. Marlowe.

"I think these are questions Jade will have to answer."

"I agree. Money doesn't make you more selfish necessarily," I said. "Yesterday, you told us just how selfish your parents were," I told Star.

"Yeah, but just writing it all down like that," she said, grimacing. "And if they disagreed, they'd stop you from being born . . . that's cold."

"What did they write down?" Misty asked. "Did they ever tell you?"

"Of course. They both throw it back in each other's faces all the time. First, they agreed that my mother would stay home for only six months and then my father would pay for the nanny afterward out of his money."

"What do you mean, out of his money?" Star asked.

"They always kept track of what each other made. They have always had separate bank accounts and they agree on what they are both responsible for like the mortgage, real estate taxes, utility bills. She has her car and he has his and they keep the expenses for each car separate. Food is shared, of course, as it's a basic maintenance expense."

Star was looking at me with her mouth open as if I really was from another planet.

"They do that to maintain their self-integrity. My

mother's not such a radical feminist, but she believes it's important for her to keep her identity and if she turns all her money over to her husband, she loses that identity, and my father certainly wouldn't turn all of his money over to her."

"So does she call herself Mrs. Lester?" Star queried with a twist in her lips.

"She uses her maiden name for her professional name, Maureen Mathews." I thought for a moment. "Often, when they sent out invitations for things, they did write Mr. Michael Lester and Ms. Maureen Mathews."

"My mother's gone back to her maiden name now," Misty said. She turned to Cat. "What about your mother?"

"Yes," she said.

"Your parents sound like they were divorced before they got married," Star muttered.

I almost laughed. It was something I had thought myself.

"Let's just say they were together but divided. Equally," I added.

"What else went into the agreement?" Misty wondered.

"After my mother returned to work, my father was to share full responsibilities for my care. If I needed to be brought to the doctor and my mother was at work, he would have to leave work. The following time, she would. The same was true for school events, dentist visits, dermatologist visits, optometrist visits, orthodontist . . ."

"We get the point," Star said.

"They actually kept track?" Misty asked.

I nodded.

"I grew up believing everyone had a large calendar on the wall in their kitchens with their father's first initial in some squares and their mother's in others. When I visited friends and didn't see their calendars, I asked and they either laughed or looked at me funny. Some admitted their parents kept small diaries for scheduled appointments, but few talked about it like I did.

"I guess that's when I began to feel a little different from some of my friends. Actually, what happened is I started to feel guilty about it all," I said.

"Why?" Cat asked and as usual looked down almost immediately.

"Because I knew my mother would rather be someplace else or my father had to shift some important meeting because he's forced to be doing things with me instead. Whenever they could when I was older, they just hired a limousine to cart me around but for quite a long time, one or the other had to be with me and there are places and meetings that require a parent to be present."

"All your expenses, they shared, right?" Misty asked.

"Almost all. There were times when my mother didn't agree about something my father had bought me or vice versa and the way they settled it was the other didn't have to contribute."

"They were always like this and you thought they were in love?" Star asked with a smirk.

"Yes, I did. I don't think they were like this from the very start. As I said, I think they were romantic and then they just became . . ."

"What?"

I looked at Dr. Marlowe. There was no doubt she was very interested in my answer. It had taken me a long time to find it, many hours of watching my parents argue and gradually become more comfortable as strangers than lovers.

"Threatened," I said.

Star looked at Misty, who shrugged.

"Can you explain what you mean, Jade?" Dr. Marlowe asked so softly, I almost didn't hear her question.

"I guess they each realized how much of themselves they would have to surrender to make the marriage work, and when I came along, the price went up. My mother was always afraid she would become less and less if she had children, and my father was always afraid he would get weaker and weaker as my mother demanded more of him."

"Is she right about all this?" Star asked Dr. Marlowe. "Does she know what she's talking about?"

"Maybe," Dr. Marlowe said.

"Don't you ever say yes or no?" Star snapped at her.

Doctor Marlowe just looked calmly at her. "Yes," she said finally, holding her expression for a moment and then we all laughed. It felt good, like we were all able to stop pulling on a rope.

From the way Star looked at me, I knew she had another delicious question rolling around in her brain.

"What about this?" she asked, motioning around the room.

"This?"

"Coming here to see the therapist. Who pays for that?"

"Oh, they both do that," I said. "Although there's no question my father thinks it's my mother's fault and my mother thinks it's my father's."

"So how did they agree on it?" Misty asked.

"The judge made them agree," I said.

"The judge made them?"

"I'm practically a ward of the state at the moment," I said. "You didn't have all that much to do with your parents' divorce, did you?"

She shook her head.

"You do?" she asked.

"Are you kidding? I have two new best friends," I told her.

"Who?" Star asked.

"My parents' lawyers," I said and I laughed.

None of the others joined me.

They were all just staring at me. Why weren't they laughing too? I wondered.

Until I felt the first tear slide down my cheek.

2

"Sometimes I wish my parents had sued each other for divorce immediately after I was born," I said after I regained control of myself. "That way I wouldn't have to live through all this. Everything would have been decided down to the last Egyptian vase or Persian rug before I even had a chance to understand that most kids have two parents living at home, parents who are not on opposite sides of a seesaw trying to outweigh each other in importance.

"What you don't have, you don't miss, I suspect. At the beginning of all this, things were not all that different from the way they are now. I used to think of myself as the golden latchkey child who returned to an empty house in which there was still a maid, a cook, and around it, a small army of grounds people cutting and pruning to keep our home looking like something special in the gated community. My parents were rarely home when I got home from school. Most of the time though, my mother would get home before my father. One day I think she decided that getting home ahead of him made it look like her job was less important, so she started to stay later and later in order to arrive home after my father.

"Then there was the division of labor. My mother discussed the menu with the cook. My father was in charge of the grounds maintenance employees. They had a business manager to help with the bills and keep the separate accounts, and everything they bought for the house they evaluated together and both had to agree to buy or it had to be bought with separate money."

"That doesn't sound like a family. It sounds like a business," Star muttered.

"You're probably right. They saw it more like a partnership with each of them holding equal shares. Maybe my family can go on the stock market, Dr. Marlowe," I said. "Lester Incorporated. Only, who'd want to invest in it since the partners don't?" I added.

She gave me that blank therapist's face, that look that made me turn to myself for the answers.

"Yes, that's what's happened," I said to Star. "You've hit it right on the head—their relationship was more like a business than a marriage. And now the company's gone bankrupt."

"You've still got plenty of money," Star said with

that now familiar twist in her lips that assured me I would find no sympathy on this subject.

"Oh, yes, plenty of money. The company's just out of that other stuff families need. You know, what's it called, Dr. Marlowe? Love?" I nodded before she could respond. "That's it. Love. We ran out of love and there just wasn't any to be had so we had to close the company doors.

"Now, the partners are fighting over the assets and I just happened to be another asset. Each of them wants to be sure he gets his fair share, you see. Well, maybe each would like to get more than his fair share. That way, he or she can claim some kind of victory. That way they won't feel so bad about the years they've invested in this business.

"And so my dear sisters, or OWP's as Misty has called us, I find myself in court where the most personal details about my life are openly displayed, renamed as exhibits and spread out on tables for lawyers, sociologists and therapists to gawk at. Do you have any idea what it's like to have to answer personal questions in the judge's office with a court stenographer taking down your every word and the judge peering at you with fish eyes?" I asked them, raising my voice.

Misty shook her head. Star stared and Cat bit her lower lip and nodded. Maybe she did know. We'd soon find out, I thought.

"I knew things were getting worse and worse before the beginning of the divorce, but I guess I either wouldn't face the possibility of their getting a divorce or I thought they wouldn't do it because of the waste of time and money. They would just continue to live through periods of war and truces until one or the other got tired of it and compromised.

"One thing about them, they didn't stop caring about public appearances, right up to the day my father's lawyer served my mother with a copy of the petition for divorce. They would get dressed up, my father in one of his stylish tuxedos and my mother in a designer gown and her diamonds, and even tell each other how nice they looked. Then they would leave, maybe not arm in arm, but together enough to give the appearance things were fine. All they had to do was tell each other how important an event was to her or his careers and they would cooperate, as if it was part of the rules of war that you didn't harm the other's professional life.

"It's weird. They still compliment each other when they speak to other people. I've heard my mother, just as recently as yesterday, brag about my father's talents and the buildings he's designed, and my father has told people how good a businesswoman my mother is. I guess they want to reassure themselves and others that they had every reason to be fooled. Anyone would have wanted my mother for a wife or my father for a husband. Talk about being civilized about hating each other," I said, shaking my head. "They smile as they shoot at each other with legal bullets."

"Your father's lawyer served your mother papers?" Cat asked. "Where?"

"What difference does that make?" Star asked, but

I thought that was a good question because the event of actually receiving such documents is traumatic. I began to wonder more about Cat's story and what had happened between her parents.

"Actually, he just mailed them to her," I said. "She received them at home and found them while she was sifting through the pile of mail with her name on it. Her professional name," I added.

"What did she do?" Star asked.

"Nothing special that night. You'd never know anything was wrong. Remember what I told you about my mother's ability to maintain the fortress of her pride? She might lose, but she's never defeated.

"They were both at dinner. I remember that meal; I remember almost every detail of that, what should I call it, that Last Supper, even though we still ate together afterward. We might even eat together tonight, but that was the last dinner where they pretended they cared enough about each other and me to keep the marriage on track.

"I remember we had chicken Kiev with wild rice. Mother had chosen the wine, a French Chardonnay. For dessert there was a deep dish apple cobbler with vanilla ice cream."

"You make it sound like a restaurant," Star said.

"It's as good as any I've been to and I've been to quite a few in New York, here and London," I said.

"You've been to London?" Misty asked.

"Of course. We were supposed to go to Paris this year. Mother claims we still will, but just she and I of course, and my father says he will take me on a business trip and has upped the bid to Paris and Madrid. Mother is now considering Venice, Madrid and Paris. It's all on hold, dependent upon the outcome of the divorce, final financial arrangements, custody, etc.," I said.

They were all giving me that look again, those wide eyes of amazement.

"Back to the Last Supper," I continued. "As I said, you'd never have known anything was wrong. My father talked about his new design project and my mother boasted that she was having lunch with the president of her company the next day. They argued a little about politics. My father is more conservative, but sometimes I think my mother disagrees with his political views just to disagree, know what I mean?"

"Yes," Misty said.

"No," Star said.

Cat shook her head.

"My parents never talked about politics," she said.

"At the Last Supper, my father complained about some work the gardeners had done on the hedges and threatened to look for a new company to take care of the property and my mother announced the need to get new patio lounges. With those kinds of topics for discussion, how was I to suspect anything? There I was eating away, living in my own private bubble as usual, my head full of plans for the next day.

"Then dessert was served and my mother, in a tone as casual as though she were still speaking about patio furniture, said that she had received papers from

Arnold Klugman, whom I knew from previous discussions about other legal matters to be my parents' attorney.

"Without a beat my father said, 'Good.'

"My mother said, 'I'll have Sheldon Fishman call him in the morning.'

" 'You're using Sheldon Fishman?' my father asked with mild interest.

" 'Judith Milner used him and was quite satisfied,' she replied.

"He nodded and returned to his dessert. When Mrs. Caron looked in on us, he complimented her on the meal and she thanked him. I went upstairs afterward to begin studying for an English exam, still not having an inkling of what was going on. I never took much interest in their legal concerns before. Why should I now? I thought."

"When did you learn what was really happening between them?" Misty asked.

"Two days later it was my mother's turn to pick me up after band rehearsal. My father had flown to Denver for a meeting and wouldn't be back until the next day. My girlfriends' mothers had picked us up all week and it was now my family's turn. The carpool arrangements made it difficult to just send a taxi and the limousine would have been overkill.

"I remember Mother was very irritable about it and constantly on the car phone, barking orders at her staff. We dropped the others off and then she pulled into our driveway, still talking on the phone. When I got out, she called for me to wait.

"She finished her conversation and got out of the car, folding her arms under her breasts and looking down as she paced around the driveway, her heels clicking like quarters falling on the black tile. I couldn't imagine what was going on. It looked like it was going to start raining any moment and I was anxious to get into the house. I wanted to call one of my girlfriends about a boy named Jeremy Brian who I thought liked me. That's how oblivious I was to the war about to begin raging around me.

" 'You know your father and I are not getting along, Jade,' my mother finally said, tossing her hair back as if the strands were annoying flies buzzing at her ear.

"So? I thought. I hadn't really noticed all that much of an escalation in their arguments, but maybe that was because I was no longer paying much attention.

" 'It's gotten worse,' she said. 'He's got his fixed ideas and his stubborn streak and I can't deal with it anymore. We've both gone to see our lawyers to do something about it.'

"My heart did flip-flops as I realized that was what they had been discussing two nights ago at dinner.

" 'What's that mean?' I asked.

" 'I want you to know, we're going to begin formal divorce procedures,' she said and looked up at me quickly. 'A no-fault, incompatibility,' she added. Before I could respond, her car phone rang and she had to pick it up and talk.

"I didn't wait around. I went inside and ran to my

room where I sat on my bed staring at the wall, wondering how anything like this could happen to me. What had happened to all the perfection? Where was my protective bubble? I was thinking about the embarrassment, of course, but I felt very frightened, too, like a bird that's been flying and flying and suddenly realizes all her feathers are gone and any moment she's going to drop to earth, hard.

"My mother came into the house but just called up to me to tell me she would talk to me more later; she had to return to work for a big meeting. She said, 'Don't worry. It will be all right. I'll take care of you.'

"She'll take care of me? I nearly broke out in hysterical laughter, but instead I sat there and cried.

"Of course, I thought the real reason they were divorcing was either my mother or my father had fallen in love with someone else and one or the other had found out. I envisioned it to be someone with whom they worked. I almost wish that was the reason now. At least I might be able to understand that better than incompatibility. How could two people who had been married as long as they had and were as smart and talented as they were not realize until now that they didn't like each other? It made no sense. It still doesn't."

"That's what I thought about my parents, too," Misty said.

"I never thought that about mine," Star added.

Cat just looked from them to me and remained her silent self.

"When my father returned from Denver the next

day, he was furious that she had told me about it all without him being present.

"I was already home from school. My mother was at work and my father came directly from his office. He knocked on my door. I was still feeling dazed and numb and had just flopped on my bed and was lying there, staring up at the ceiling.

" 'Hi,' he said. 'How are you doing?'

" 'Peachy keen,' I told him.

"I wasn't any angrier at him than I was at her. I was furious at both of them for failing. You know," I said, pausing in my tale, "that's something I've been wanting to throw up at them for some time now. Parents have so many expectations for us, demands, requirements, whatever. We have to behave and do well in school and be sure to make them proud of us and never embarrass them. We have to be decent and respectful and respectable, but why is it that they can go and destroy the family and drag us through all this to satisfy themselves?

"What about that, Dr. Marlowe?"

"It's a fair question to put to them," she said.

Star laughed.

"My momma and daddy would just feel awful if I asked them," she said. "First, I'd have to find them and get Momma while she was sober enough to understand."

"I thought of that question, too," Misty said. "I just haven't asked it."

I looked at Cat and she looked away quickly. What *was* her story?

"My father didn't even seem to recognize my anger. He had his own to express first," I said, getting back to my story.

" 'We were supposed to do this together,' he said, 'but it's just like her to do what she did. Just in character for her to take control. Don't you worry. It's been duly noted,' he assured me. He was already keeping a legal diary for his lawyer to use in court."

I sighed, crossed my legs and sat back.

"So from the very beginning, the divorce was to be bitter and I was the battleground. Suddenly, I, who had been nothing but an inconvenience, became important, but believe me, I wasn't flattered. On occasion, I've told both my parents they shouldn't love me so much. They both looked confused, but I think deep down in their hearts, they knew what I meant, they knew what they'd buried.

"Dinner that evening was under a cloud, but neither of them would give the other the satisfaction of knowing he or she was terribly upset. They ate like there was no tomorrow just to demonstrate that nothing had damaged their appetites. Neither noticed I hardly ate at all.

"Their conversation was limited to the most essential things and there was a new formal tone to both of their voices, but before the dinner ended, both directed themselves to me, asking me questions about school, about the band, about an upcoming dance I was sure they had forgotten until now. One would ask a question and the other would try to top it by asking for more detail.

"Suddenly, they were both trying to impress me with their concern and interest in my life and my affairs. I should have realized then that they were going to fight over custody, but as I said, I just assumed that if they really went through with the divorce, my mother and I would remain at the house and my father would live someplace else.

"The friends I had in school whose parents had divorced all lived with their mothers and had regular visits with their fathers, and like you guys, none of them talked much about the actual divorce proceedings. They were far more protected from the unpleasant parts than I would be.

"What was supposed to happen next was the lawyers were to get together and work things out. They did work out almost everything else but me and that affected all the other compromises. When it came to the question of custody, the war began. I think that took my mother by surprise, which my father enjoyed. I didn't know about that aspect yet. I just heard bits and pieces about their financial issues, the battle over what assets were joint and what were separate. Since my mother wasn't claiming any physical or emotional abuse, my father was permitted to remain in the house. At least they didn't have to work out any kind of visitation schedule for the time being.

"But a regular trial would have to take place for the judge to decide who should get custody of me. I realized pretty quickly that my opinions, my answers to the judge's questions, would all play a big role and that was why my parents were suddenly . . ."

"What?" Misty asked.

I stared at her for a moment as the words played in my head, waiting for the right one. It seemed so obvious.

"Parents," I replied.

"Huh?"

"She means a momma and daddy and not two business partners," Star explained.

"Exactly," I said, smiling. I looked at Dr. Marlowe. She seemed very pleased.

"That should have made you happy," Misty said.

Once again I glanced at Dr. Marlowe because I knew she would be interested in my reply.

"It does and it doesn't," I said. "I mean I like the attention and all, but I hate feeling that I'm getting it only so that they can each feel that they're outdoing the other. It's like having something nice that's also bad, like, like eating your favorite ice cream but it's so cold, it hurts your teeth."

They all looked confused.

"I guess I'm not making any sense," I said, sitting back. "That's why I didn't even want to start this."

"You're making sense," Misty said. She looked at Star.

"Yeah, you're making sense," Star agreed.

Cat nodded.

"A lot of sense," she said in a voice just a shade above a whisper, "even though it's confusing."

"Huh?"

"That's why we're here, to find a way to live with it," Cat continued and for the first time in three days, all of us looked at her as someone who could bring something to this beside shyness, fear and silence.

Before anyone could speak however, we heard the rattle of glasses and heavy footsteps in the hallway outside the office door.

"Lemonade!" Dr. Marlowe's sister Emma cried and came walking in, carrying a silver tray on which she had a jug of freshly made lemonade and four glasses with a plate of cookies.

"I hope I'm not too early, Dr. Marlowe," Emma said, looking afraid she had interrupted. We all thought it was amusing that she called her sister Dr. Marlowe. Misty suggested she might be a client of her own sister, but I thought that was some sort of a conflict of interest or something.

"No, you're right on schedule, Emma. Thank you."

Emma's plump cheeks rose as her lips formed a rosebud smile. She placed the tray on the table and stepped back.

"Everyone looks so bright and cheery today. It is a pretty day. I hope you'll give them time to enjoy some of it, Doctor. Young girls need sunshine," she recited as if it was some ancient truth.

"I will, Emma. Thank you."

She nodded, flashed another smile at us and left. I think all of us were wondering for a moment if that might be the way we would be years from now. How deep were Emma's wounds in comparison to ours and what happens if you can't mend, really and truly mend?

Will we always be this angry and afraid of forever failing at relationships and therefore always be terrified of being forever lonely? You didn't have to be a psychiatrist to see that loneliness was Emma's problem. It was like some disease affecting her smile, her laugh, her very movement.

"Help yourselves, girls," Dr. Marlowe said and we did. "I'll be right back. I have to check on lunch," she said and left.

Dr. Marlowe is very smart giving us these breaks, I thought. It's too exhausting otherwise.

"Where do you live?" I asked Cat as I reached for a cookie and lemonade.

"Pacific Palisades," she replied. She nibbled on her cookie.

"Where do you go to school?"

"I go to a parochial school," she said. She brushed back her hair.

"I see you cut your hair," I told her and she nodded.

"I did it myself."

"It's an improvement," I said, "but you should try to get your mother to take you over to Patty's on Rodeo."

She stared at me as if I spoke a foreign language.

"That's Rodeo as in Rodeo Drive," I said. "You know if you have a good stylist work on it, your face won't look as chubby."

"Maybe she doesn't think she looks chubby. Maybe she's happy with how she looks," Star said.

"I'm just trying to be helpful."

"Sometimes people can be too helpful."

"That's ridiculous. No one can be too helpful," I said.

"People who are always sticking their noses into other people's business are too helpful," she countered.

"I don't agree. I'm not sticking my nose into anyone's business. I'm giving her the benefit of my experience and my knowledge."

"Maybe she doesn't want it. You ever think of that?"

"Of course she wants it. Don't you, Cathy?" I asked her, practically pleading for her to agree.

She looked like she would cry.

"Don't you see that you're doing the same thing to her that your parents are doing to you?" Misty asked.

"What?"

"Trying to get her to take sides," she said.

I stared at her for a moment and then sat back. Star glared at me, and Cathy quietly ate her cookie, her eyes fixed on her lemonade.

Actually, Misty wasn't wrong. There had been something in my voice that reminded me of how my parents spoke to me now, that pleading to get me to agree with one or the other.

"She's right. I'm sorry," I said. "I was really trying to be helpful. I guess I should learn when to keep my mouth shut."

"Amen," Star said.

"You're not perfect," I charged.

"I'm not? Why bless my soul. I thought considering my wonderful home life and upbringing, I was a thing to behold," she said.

Misty laughed.

So did I.

Just as Dr. Marlowe returned.

"Well, I'm glad everyone's getting along so well," she said, and that made us all laugh, even Cat.

3

"Once my parents decided to do battle over custody, the beautifully carved figures on the civilized chess board of divorce changed to tiny knives they tried to stick into each other," I said. "In other words, things got nastier and nastier until today they rarely speak directly to each other. Civility hangs by a thin thread. What will become of me?" I declared in the voice of a Southern belle, like Scarlett O'Hara in *Gone With the Wind.* Misty laughed.

"Sometimes, if I'm in the same room with the both of them, my mother will say, 'Jade, please tell your father we're having trouble with the garbage disposal,' and my father will respond gruffly with, 'Tell her I already know about it and I'm taking care of it.' "

"So you really don't tell either of them what the other said, right?" Misty asked.

"Right. I'm like a filter through which the words they direct toward each other now have to go. I don't think I've ever had to actually repeat anything. As long as the words are directed toward me, it's all right."

"I couldn't stand that for very long," Star said. "I know it's miserable when they're spitting hate at each other, but I don't like being in the middle."

"Me neither. One day last week when they were having a conversation through me, I put my hands over my ears and I started to scream 'Leave me alone! Stop filling me up with all this garbage!'

"I thought I might tear the hair right out of my head. I know I was so red in the face I felt like I had a fever, but instead of worrying about what I was going through, they just began attacking each other.

" 'Look what you're doing to her,' my father accused.

" 'Me? It's you. You're the one who's putting us all through this ridiculous legal charade. Do you really think for one moment any judge in his right mind is going to grant you custody?'

" 'If he's in his right mind, that's all he can do,' my father responded.

"I turned and ran out of the room. I could hear them shouting at each other for a few more minutes. It was like the winding down of a storm, the slow rolling of thunder farther and farther toward the horizon until there was nothing but the drip, drip, drip of my own tears."

"I don't know how they continue to live in the same house," Misty said, shaking her head.

"Where does your father sleep now?" Star asked.

"In one of the guest rooms. That was something else that caused problems. He asked me to help move his clothing into the guest room. I didn't want to see that happening, but I didn't think it was any big deal for me to help him. Of course, as I did, he complained about my mother more and more and then she came home and saw me helping him and went ballistic.

" 'How can you help that man? Are you taking his side in this?' she screamed at me.

" 'I'm just carrying in some clothes and personal things for him,' I told her.

"That night, perhaps feeling threatened, she suddenly decided she and I had to go out to dinner. It was the first of the poisonings," I said.

"Poisonings?" Cat asked, jumping on my word, but then she looked guiltily at Star and Misty as if she had taken their assigned lines or something.

"I don't think she means she and her mother actually poisoned her father's food or anything," Misty said. Before I could respond she thought for a moment, the doubt shading her eyes, and asked, "Right?"

"Right," I said, "although I often wonder if that could be far behind. No, the kind of poisoning I mean is one planting unpleasant things about the other in my head. They're both treating my head like a garden of hate these days.

"Anyway, I couldn't remember a time before when my mother wanted to just be with me, to take me to lunch or to dinner and have a real mother-daughter conversation. Oh, I went shopping with her lots of times and we ended up having lunch at the mall or something, but most of the time, one of her girlfriends was with us or she talked about herself and her career. There wasn't anything really mother-daughter about it.

"It was funny, but when she asked me to go to dinner with her that first night, I felt bad for my father. I knew, of course, that it was a deliberate effort to exclude him, but all I could do is imagine him home alone at that big dining room table looking at all the empty chairs while Mrs. Caron served one of her gourmet meals.

"My mother made reservations for us in one of the more expensive Beverly Hills restaurants. She told me to get dressed up because we were going to an elegant place.

" 'I was after your father to take me to this restaurant for months before we started the divorce proceedings,' she explained as soon as we left the house.

" 'Why didn't he take you?' I asked.

" 'Why? You'd have to ask him and I'm sure he'll come up with some lame excuse like I was the one who was too busy or something.'

"She turned to me and smiled.

" 'You look very pretty,' she said. 'I'm glad you're wearing your hair that way, and I'm happy I bought that Vivienne Tam. It complements your figure.'

"I didn't know what to say. My mother didn't spend all that much time talking about style of clothes and hair with me very much before this. The truth was I picked out most of my clothes when I went shopping with my friends. When I went shopping with my mother she didn't give me enough time to try things on. She always wanted to get it over with quickly. She dresses stylishly herself, but she doesn't hide the fact that she thinks shopping is a waste of time. She did help me with my make-up because that was her area of expertise, being a sales manager for the cosmetics company, but she always spoke to me as if I was some client or customer in a department store.

" 'Of course,' my mother said still harping on my dress, 'your father didn't want me to buy that even though you wanted it so much. He thought it was way too expensive for a girl your age.'

" 'I don't remember that,' I said.

" 'Oh, yes. It's true. I had to pay for it myself out of my own money. I'll show you the canceled check if you like,' she told me. 'Don't be surprised,' she continued. 'Most of the nice things you have, you have because of me. I'm not the penny pincher in this family. He inherited that . . . that frugal way from his parents. You know what it's like to get a nickel out of Grandfather and Grandmother Lester. Look at the things they buy you for your birthdays. Most grandparents would have set aside some trust money for their granddaughter in a good interest-bearing account by now,' she said.

" 'But they have other grandchildren,' I said.

" 'So? They're not any more generous with your cousins. What are they going to do, take it with them and spend it in the grave? You know what they gave us for a wedding present? A five-hundred-dollar savings bond. That's right,' she said laughing, 'a savings bond. I think it's still in the safety deposit box. I get half of that and don't worry, I'll be sure I get it. If he so much as takes out one nickel from that safety deposit box . . . ,' she muttered, her lips nearly whitening in rage. She suddenly turned back to me with a smile.

" 'Oh, but I don't want you to worry about money, Jade. We're not going to end up like so many poor women and children,' she assured me. 'The fact is I have a better lawyer than he has. I should know. Arnold was my lawyer once. He doesn't have as much courtroom experience as my attorney. The fact is, I was surprised your father didn't look for a more experienced divorce attorney, a specialist like I have to get what I want and protect what you have.'

" 'I don't think Daddy wants to see me have less,' I made the mistake of saying.

"Her eyes looked like they were going to explode in her head. My mother is a very attractive woman. Her hair is just a little darker than mine and she wears it with a little sweep over her forehead like those actresses from the forties, the Veronica Lake look. She has blue-green eyes. They're more green when she gets angry. I know she's beautiful because every time I've gone places with her, I've noticed the way men turn their heads and even women look up at her with that *Why can't that be me?* expression on their faces.

"She doesn't do anything special to keep her figure

either. Once a week she might go to the fitness center, but she claims hard work, being constantly on the go, and watching her diet is all she needs to do.

"She's about an inch shorter than I am. If she was two or three inches taller, I bet she could have been a model, not that she would have wanted to be," I quickly added.

"Why not?" Star asked.

"She thinks they're just meat on the hoof, that men treat them with less respect, regardless of how much they get paid. And they have a short professional life. If you're a career woman in business, your looks don't determine how long you'll be working or how fast you will be promoted."

"Don't believe it," Star muttered.

"Don't believe what?"

"That looks don't matter. They always matter."

I glanced at Cat. She kept her eyes down the whole time Star and I argued.

"If you have skills and talent, you will get to where you want to go, to where you deserve to go," I told Star.

"Men are always going to promote women who are prettier first," she insisted.

"What would you know about it? You've never had a job or been in the business world."

"I know what men want," she said dryly.

"Oh please." I looked at Misty, who just shrugged. From what she had told us, I knew her mother had never done a day's work. She wouldn't know either, I realized.

"You watch too many soap operas," I snapped.

"Soap operas?" Star laughed. "Half the time the television doesn't work or if it does, Rodney's glued to it, watching cartoons. We only have one set in our house," she pointed out. "I bet you have five."

I thought for a moment. We had seven, but I didn't say so.

"My mother," I continued deciding to ignore Star's interruption, "is not one of those women who look prettier or more radiant when they get angry. She looks . . . scary, at least to me.

" 'Believe me,' she cried, 'your father is not concerned about your getting less or more. He has his own agenda in this divorce and you and I are not at the top of the list. Why do you think he's fighting so hard to win custody? Because he wants to be responsible for you, to be burdened by your needs? Hardly. It's a negotiations ploy, that's what it is.'

" 'What's that mean?' I asked.

"She was quiet for a moment, nodding to herself and smiling before turning to me.

" 'He thinks I'm not as smart as he is. Most men make that mistake, but I've been in plenty of negotiations with men and I know how the opponent thinks and maneuvers,' she said.

"I hated the idea of her referring to my father as the opponent, but I could see that's what he was to her now, nothing more.

" 'He thinks if he carries this ridiculous motion for custody to court and we actually have a trial date scheduled, I'll give in to his financial demands and take less.'

" 'I thought the money part was all just about settled,' I said.

" 'It would have been if there wasn't this wrinkle,' she replied. That's what I was now, a wrinkle.

" 'I don't understand,' I said.

" 'He makes more money than I do. I want my share of that as well,' she explained. 'I'm entitled to it and there are other assets that he thinks are only his. Then, there's the house. Eventually, it all will be worked out, but until then, he's playing this new game.'

" 'What am I, a checker on a checker board?' I asked.

" 'Exactly,' she said. 'I'm glad you understand. I knew you would. We've got to be more like sisters now than mother and daughter, sisters fighting the same cause, hating men who are selfish and who will belittle us,' she told me.

"But in my mind, I saw her treating me like a checker on that board as well. I just didn't say it then. I was afraid her anger might drive us off the road if I did.

"As soon as we arrived at the restaurant, my mother became the mother I knew most of my life. She claimed she had brought me there to have a heart-to-heart, but she spent most of her time talking to people she knew in the business world. In between she had to explain who all these people were and why it was so important to touch base with them, as she put it.

"When would she touch base with me? I wondered."

"Why didn't you ask her instead of wonder?" Star questioned.

"I don't know. You're right, of course. I should have confronted her then and there, but I didn't. I ate; I listened and I found myself drifting away, like some shadow of myself, becoming more and more invisible. That's what this divorce does to me, it makes me invisible, no matter what they say about how important I am.

"Every once in a while, my mother would return to the subject of our family crisis and rant about my father as if she just remembered she was in the middle of this legal action to end their marriage. She drank more than I had ever seen her drink. Usually, one martini was enough for my mother, but she was lit up like a movie marquee, advertising her anger, her determination and her pride, so she drank another and then nearly half of a third.

"Her eyes looked droopy to me by the time they served dessert. Suddenly, she was so weird. She was just staring at me and she reached across the table and took my hand.

" 'Jade,' she said, her eyes tearing up, 'we've got to stick together on this. You don't know half of what I've been through these past few years. Your father is so different from the man I married. He's obsessed with himself, with his work. Nothing matters more, not you, not me, nothing,' she said.

"She pulled herself up, took a deep breath and said, 'My attorney is going to want to speak with you very soon. I want you to be cooperative and answer all his questions as fully as you can and keep in mind the things I've told you tonight.'

" 'What sort of questions?' I wanted to know.

" 'Questions about our life, your life. They won't be hard questions. Just answer them and remember, Jade, in the end I'll always be here for you.'

"I was afraid to ride home with her. I thought we might be stopped and she would be arrested for DWI, but somehow we made it home. In the hallway, she hugged me once. It was something she hadn't done for a really long time.

"It made me cry and made my stomach ache. I didn't want her to be so sad, but I didn't want to hate my father either. I had a lot of trouble falling asleep that night.

"Despite how much she had drunk at dinner, my mother was up as early as usual the following morning. In fact, she left before I went down for breakfast. She had some meeting in San Francisco and had to fly up there for the day.

"I didn't feel like getting up and going to school. My head felt so heavy and I was exhausted from tossing about, swimming from one nightmare island to another. I decided I would stay home and just rest.

"There was a knock on my door and my father peered in.

" 'Still in bed?' he asked. He was dressed in his jacket and tie, looking as spruced up as ever.

"My father is more than just handsome. He's . . . distinguished, like a United States senator or an ambassador. He's about six feet two and has just a touch of gray at his temples which, along with his perennial tan, brings out the soft aqua blue in his eyes.

"I've always looked up to my father, thought of him as someone special, like a celebrity. He's been in the newspapers a lot, and magazines have featured his buildings and put his picture in the articles.

"He has always seemed strong and successful to me. It was one thing to see him angry and firm with my mother, but another to see him sad and weak with me.

"He came into my room and sat on my bed, lowering his head like a flag in defeat and folding his arms on his legs as he wove his fingers through each other. He stared down at the floor for a long moment.

" 'I'm sorry you have to go through all this,' he began. 'I don't want you to dislike your mother and I especially don't want you to dislike me. I know she's probably been working on you, trying to get you to take sides.'

"He looked up at me quickly to see if he was right and I had to look away which was the same as admitting it was true.

" 'I know she's doing that and it's cruel and wrong of her. She's not herself these days. She's intent on getting her way and that's all that matters to her.'

" 'Why?' I asked.

"He studied me for a moment and nodded as if he had decided I was old enough or smart enough to understand.

" 'For some reason,' he said, 'defeating me makes her feel more like a woman of substance, it strengthens her self-image. I can't tell you why she feels that way. I haven't done much to frustrate her ambitions, have I? She wanted a full-time executive position with her firm. I said fine. Go ahead. I won't stand in your way. I'll pay for nannies and servants and do whatever is necessary to let you pursue your professional goals.

" 'But it wasn't enough for her. She wanted more. She wanted to dominate. You know how the Mathewses are,' he continued, now talking about her parents. 'Her father and mother's pictures are right beside *snob* in the dictionary. I never told you how badly I was treated by them when we were courting. I was just starting out and of course, no one could predict whether I would be successful or not. And my family didn't have a high enough social standing for them, either. To this day they still think your mother has married below her station in society.

" 'She can't help herself. She's inherited too much of that,' he added.

"He reached for my hand and looked me in the eyes and said, 'I don't want you to become a Mathews snob, Jade. You have a lot more than most girls do, but it's no reason for you to look down on anyone and lose out on real friendships. Just think,' he said dropping some of the poison seeds into the garden, 'does your mother have any real friends, any close friends? Anyone she knows and pals around with these days is just as snobby or even snobbier than she is.

" 'I just know that if I move out and leave you behind, you'll be worse off. I'm not going to permit it to happen,' he assured me.

" 'Soon my attorney will ask to meet with you. You've met Arnold before on social occasions, so you know you don't have to be afraid of him or his questions,' my father said.

"Here I go again, I thought.

" 'What sort of questions?' I asked.

" 'Simple questions about your life. Just answer everything honestly,' he said and rose smiling. 'It will be easy and all this unpleasantness will be cleared up.'

" 'All this unpleasantness?' Was that all it was to him, just some unpleasantness? To me it was utter disaster.

" 'I know you can't be enjoying it,' he said. He started out. 'Say,' he said from the doorway, turning back to me, 'why don't you pop over to my office this afternoon after school. I'd like to show you the model of my last project. You'd probably enjoy seeing it. It's a four-hundred-million-dollar project. You'll be proud of your dad when you see what's involved,' he said.

"I couldn't remember the last time my father had invited me to his office. In fact, I think I had been there less than a half a dozen times. He has beautiful offices on the twenty-first floor of a building on Wilshire Boulevard. The view from his office is spectacular. You can see the ocean and on clear days, Catalina Island.

" 'I'm not going to school today,' I said just before

he closed the door behind him. 'I have a bad headache.'

" 'Oh?' he said, looking at me with concern. 'How long has this been going on?'

" 'About three months,' I replied, pinpointing the date of the Last Supper.

"He studied me and then nodded.

" 'That's why I want to put an end to this stupidity as quickly as I can. Your mother puts up a big front, but she'll be happier being totally free,' he added. 'It's what she wants. Unfortunately, it's who she is,' he added and left, leaving me feeling as if he had taken all the oxygen out of my room along with him.

"Later, I was sorry I stayed home from school. There is nothing more dreary than an empty house filled with the echoes of people fighting and hissing at each other like a pair of snakes. The walls, the shadows in every corner, the bong of the grandfather clock, the long whistle of a tea kettle, every sight and every sound seemed hollow. I felt like I was on the set of a movie. Nothing was real to me anymore. All the pictures of them together that still hung on walls or were in frames on tables were illusions. Even the family photos looked phony.

"All these smiles, I thought, were false. Suddenly my parents' faces resembled balloons that had lost air, whereas I felt I was floating away, drifting into the wind, belonging nowhere anymore, like you three," I said, looking from Cat to Misty to Star, "an orphan with parents."

I took a deep breath and held my head back to keep

the tears from slipping down my face. Cat cleared her throat. Everyone was looking at me, waiting.

"So," I continued, smiling, "now it really began. Two days later, my mother picked me up at school and brought me to her attorney's office.

" 'You didn't tell your father about this, did you?' she asked me as soon as I got into the car.

" 'No,' I said, but I hadn't told her about him planning to schedule a meeting between me and Arnold Klugman, his attorney, either.

" 'Good,' she said. 'Not that we have to hide anything. It's just better this way.'

"Better for whom? I thought. Certainly not for me. I was literally trembling as if I were in Aspen in February without a jacket or boots."

"Where?" Star asked.

"Aspen. It's a place where a lot of rich and famous people go skiing," Misty said.

"Well, excuse me. I haven't even seen snow up close much less slid down a hill on stupid sticks," she muttered.

"Have you ever read the fable of the Fox and the Grapes?" I asked her.

"No, why?"

"You might appreciate it. This fox is trying desperately to get his mouth on these grapes on the vine only they're too high and he can't get to them so he turns around and says, 'They're probably sour anyway.' "

She glared at me.

"Your father might be right about that snob thing," she said.

"I'm not a snob, but I'm not ashamed of what I have and who I am," I said.

"What was it like at the lawyer's?" Misty asked quickly to stop any more bickering.

"It was horrible," I said. "Her attorney has these really plush offices in Beverly Hills. I took a look around at the three secretaries, the rich oak paneling, the expensive paintings and rugs and thought the divorce business must be pretty good. Everyone treated my mother as if she was the most important client they had. She loves all that stroking. I guess she should have been born into royalty. What a waste of regal posture and dignity.

"Her attorney, Mr. Fishman, was a tall, lean man with beady dark eyes and heavy eyebrows. He had a smile that reminded me of ice because it slid on and off his face so easily. After my mother introduced us, he asked me to take the seat in front of his large, dark cherry wood desk and then after my mother sat, he sat and rubbed his palms together before clapping his hands once like some magician who was going to lift a black velvet cloth to reveal the missing diamond or the end to this marital madness that was destroying us all.

" 'Well, Jade,' he began, 'you know your mother has hired me to help her get through this very difficult situation. Divorce is never pleasant, and your mother wants to make every effort to see that you come through this unscathed.'

"He looked at my mother to see if she approved of the way he had begun and she smiled.

" 'Jade is a very bright and mature young lady,' my mother told him. 'She'll do what has to be done and do it well.'

" 'I'm sure she will,' he said with that chilly smile.

"I kept thinking I'm sure he doesn't really care. I said nothing. I stared at him and waited.

" 'What I want to do today is make you aware of what is going to happen and what you will be asked to do,' he said. 'The judge is going to have a psychologist evaluate your family situation to produce a custodial assessment. We have learned today that Dr. Thelma Morton will perform the evaluation. I am familiar with her. She is a very competent and fair-minded person and I think you will like her. Besides her testimony, there will be testimony from some of your mother's friends and someone from your school.'

" 'Who?' I demanded.

"He looked at his folder for a moment.

" 'Your guidance counselor, a Miss Bickerstaff,' he said.

" 'Why her?' I asked. I didn't particularly like her. I thought she was cold and officious and I had always suspected that she didn't really like being around young people.

" 'She and I have met on two occasions for parent-teacher conferences,' my mother explained. Your father couldn't be there either time even though they were both very important meetings, remember?'

"Neither she nor my father had been to the last

meeting, the one where colleges were being discussed, I thought.

" 'So we have your school officials, family and friends, and Dr. Morton,' Mr. Fishman catalogued. 'They will be the witnesses in the courtroom. The judge relies on their testimony a great deal, and of course, on what you will say to him.

" 'I can tell you right now,' he said, 'because of your age, he'll most assuredly ask you which of your parents you preferred to have custody and why. Most likely,' he added, seeing the look on my face, 'this will occur in camera, which means privately, usually with a court reporter present. It's rare for a child, even a teenager, to testify at trial,' he said flashing that cold grin at me.

" 'You can't be pressured,' my mother commented, obviously referring to the fact that my father would not be present during the interview with the judge.

"Is she for real? I thought. What is all this if not pressure?"

"I'm glad I didn't have to do that," Misty said.

"I'm not. If a judge had asked me, I would have told him I didn't want either one of my parents to have custody," Star said.

Cat's eyes flashed in silent agreement.

" 'Do you understand everything so far?' Mr. Fishman asked me.

"I shrugged. It wasn't calculus. What was there to understand? I knew what he wanted me to do and I didn't like it.

" 'In all my custody cases, and I have had a number, actually more than ever recently,' he added, nodding at my mother, 'I like to meet like this in a casual way with the child or children,' he explained, sitting back and pressing his long fingers into a cathedral.

"Casual? I thought looking around at his impressive office, the walls covered in books and plaques with framed degrees. Hardly casual.

" 'What I'd really appreciate hearing are your concerns,' he said.

"I simply stared at him coldly. He looked to my mother.

" 'Maybe you'd feel more comfortable speaking if it were just you and I,' he said, swinging his eyes conspiratorially to my mother and then back to me.

" 'Actually, I'd feel less comfortable,' I told him. That icy smile returned, stiffer, colder.

" 'I appreciate how difficult this is for you,' he said. 'Let me assure you it's not our intention to drive your father completely out of your life. Your mother has no opposition to reasonable visitations, trips, vacations.

" 'What we want to do,' he continued, 'is maintain as much normalcy in your life as possible under these trying circumstances. You're comfortable in your home, comfortable with your world as it is right now, correct?'

" 'Hardly,' I told him.

" 'I don't mean the confrontational atmosphere. I'd like you to stop for a moment and try to separate yourself from that and ask yourself how can you best keep the good things about your life, your world? Just think about that, okay? And when you are asked questions by others, think how your answers will support that, okay?'

"I looked at my mother.

" 'I'm not losing the house,' she said firmly. 'No matter what he and Arnold say.'

" 'You won't,' Mr. Fishman assured her.

"She looked at me as if that was the point. If she keeps the house, then won't I want her to have custody so I could stay in my room? As if my room, my things were all that mattered, I thought.

" 'Let me give you an idea of what sort of questions you might be asked,' Mr. Fishman continued. 'Think hard. Who seems to be around more when you need advice? With whom would you rather share your most intimate thoughts, your problems? Who understands you more? Who's been there for you more?

" 'You don't have all that much longer to go before you're an independent person, Jade. Think about what would be best for you in finishing out your dependence on your parents. Most importantly, don't think of this as if you're choosing one over the other. No one's asking you to love your father less or your mother more. You might just help make a decision that's better for them, too.

" 'You don't want to end up being a burden to your father,' he interjected. 'He's a very busy and creative man. He needs his mind free of worry.'

"I felt like two snakes had come alive in my stomach, the snakes that had replaced my parents in the house, and they were slithering over each other and under each other until they had tied their bodies tightly around one another and formed a painfully poisonous knot in my stomach, a knot so tight neither could unravel it. Instead, they panicked and pulled and tugged on each other, tearing each other apart and it was all happening inside me.

"Mr. Fishman must have seen something of this in my face. He very astutely looked at my mother and then smiled and said, 'Fine. This is a good start. We'll talk again.'

"He and my mother stood up, but my legs felt like they had turned to rubber. I actually wobbled.

"Mr. Fishman came around the desk and took my arm.

" 'Are you all right?' he asked me. His voice sounded far away, down at the bottom of a well, echoing.

" 'I feel a little nauseated,' I said. The bubbles were building in my stomach.

"They took me out to the bathroom quickly. I went into the stall and threw up in the toilet while my mother ran the sink to cover up the sound of my heaving and kept asking if I was all right.

"Finally, I came out.

" 'I'll take you to the doctor,' she said. 'You probably caught a bug.'

" 'I'll be all right,' I told her. 'I just want to go home and lie down.'

" 'Damn him to hell for doing this,' she muttered. 'Damn him.'

"I kept my eyes closed most of the time in the car and wished I could shut my ears as she rambled on about what my father was doing to us. I couldn't wait to get upstairs and into my room. I got undressed and into bed quickly and when she looked in on me later, I kept my eyes closed and pretended to be asleep.

"Mrs. Caron came up with a bowl of chicken soup. I ate a little, and the nausea subsided and a headache took its place. I began to wonder if my mother had been right and I had caught a bug. Maybe I should have gone to the doctor.

"Later, when my father came home and learned I had missed dinner and was in bed, he stopped by.

"He wanted to know what was wrong and I told him I had stomach trouble and a headache.

" 'Why didn't she take you to a doctor? Did she have some meeting that she had to go to instead?' he demanded. My headache got worse. 'Just come knocking on my door tonight if you don't feel any better, Jade. I'll call Harry Weinstein and he'll see you no matter what time it is. She was probably worried she'd have to spend time in a waiting room.'

" 'No,' I said. 'I didn't want to go.'

" 'When you're sick, you don't know what's best for you. That's what parents are for,' he declared.

"Where was he when I had the measles? I wondered. He was in Toronto at an architects' convention. And where was he when I had the flu so bad I lost nearly ten pounds? He was in Boston building an office complex. My mother was in Atlanta at a major corporate meeting.

"Lots of times, I thought, I had to be the one who knew what was best for me, sick or not.

"You were right before, Star," I said. "I want to run away. That night it was all I could think about.

"And later, I did."

"You did?" Misty asked. I remembered she had tried to do that, too.

"What happened?" Cat asked.

I stared at her for a moment. I was almost ashamed to tell them.

I gathered up my courage and told them the truth. "No one noticed."

4

"It took me a while to decide I was really going to run away. First, I didn't know where I would go. I would never want to go to any of my relatives. I never got along with my cousins on my father's side, and I had no relationship whatsoever with my uncles and aunts. My grandparents would just send me back, special delivery, in fact," I said.

Misty laughed.

"Whether or not I ran off wasn't going to be determined by having enough money. After the filing of divorce papers, my parents fell over themselves to set up a checking account for me, supposedly so I could learn how to be independent. There was also some psychological mumbo-jumbo about giving me a sense of security at a critical time in my emotional and psychological development," I added with a side glance at Dr. Marlowe.

"Years ago, they had decided that there might be occasions when I would need money and they would both be away on business. It had happened a few times. So they set up an arrangement at their bank to be sure I could get up to five hundred dollars out of their accounts anytime I needed it. I never did, but the opportunity was always there.

"Now, they both contributed a thousand dollars to a checking account of my own, and, in almost a ceremonial manner, presented me with the checkbook and ATM card after dinner one night. Dinners had become like wakes, with their marriage lying in a casket right beside the dining room table. At this point it was rare to hear either of them say, 'We agree,' on anything, but my father reached into his inside jacket pocket after dessert had been served, cleared his throat, glanced at my mother and began as if he were the master of ceremonies on a dais at a banquet. I imagined him tapping his spoon against the glass to get my mother's and my attention.

" 'Jade,' he said, 'your mother and I have decided that you are old enough now to have control of your own finances. You have to learn how to manage money. Someday you'll have a great deal of it. Hopefully, most of it will come from your own efforts and not only from what you inherit,' he added with a smile.

"My mother just pressed her lips together and stared down at the table, making little circles in the tablecloth with her forefingers.

" 'Anyway, recognizing this need, your mother and I have agreed to open this account for you. You have only to go to the bank at your convenience and finish this signature card to be able to write checks and use the ATM card. It's an interest-bearing account. We both thought that would be economically wise since we don't anticipate you'll be writing very many checks. Anyway,' he said, 'without any more talk, here's your checkbook and your ATM card.'

"He rose and brought it to me. I looked at the checkbook, saw the two thousand dollar balance and looked up at him and then my mother, surprised at the amount. Everything I needed was paid for: clothes, food, transportation. On what would I spend my two thousand dollars? New CD's, magazines?"

"I would have loved to have had that problem," Star grumbled.

" 'We each put in a thousand dollars,' my mother wanted me to know and then she added, 'but since he makes more than I do, proportionately, I've obviously put in more than my share.'

" 'Now that's not a fair statement,' my father countered. 'You never asked that I contribute any more than you—proportionately or otherwise.'

" 'It's just common sense, Michael. With all your business sense, you should know that without anyone having to point it out to you.'

"My father's stiff, regal posture softened as if he had been punched in the stomach.

" 'Do you want me to put in more?' he asked.

" 'Do what you think is right, Michael,' she said, shifting her eyes toward me with that conspiratorial look. I knew she wanted me to remember all the things she had said about my father's family and their tendency to be frugal.

"My father looked very uncomfortable, as if he had been trapped. It was like every sentence, every move each of them made was a well-thought-out strategy to make the other look bad in my eyes. I felt as if they were already in court, jousting with lances dipped in venom.

" 'Why didn't you bring this up before you had me present her with the checkbook and card, Maureen?'

" 'Why should I have to?' she threw back.

"He glanced at me. I could see he was absolutely raging inside. I could see his face turning more and more crimson as if there were a fire under his cheeks.

" 'I'll have the accountant work out what is proportionately accurate and add whatever has to be added immediately,' my father promised me.

" 'I don't care,' I said. 'I don't want anyone's money,' I added. I wanted to say more. I wanted to say I want my life to go back to what it was. I want you to act like you love each other again and stop all this bickering. I want the war to end. I had all that on the tip of my tongue, but I felt my throat close up and a lump like a small lead ball settle on my heart. I was glad that dinner was over. 'I've got homework to do,' I said. 'May I be excused?'

" 'Of course,' my mother said.

"I rose and started away. My father called to me.

" 'You might as well hold on to all of this until it's proportionately corrected,' he said as snidely as he could. He held out the checkbook and ATM card and I snatched it out of his hand and practically ran up to my room.

"When I got there, I threw the checkbook across the room. I retrieved it before I went to sleep and when I decided to run off, it came in handy. By then, my father had added an additional seven hundred and fifty dollars and I had gone to the bank and registered the signature card."

Star whistled.

"That's a lot of pocket money, girl."

I thought for a moment, sipped some lemonade, and then sat back. The miniature grandfather clock ticked. For a moment the numbers looked blurry to me. You really get to hate time when the world around you is crumbling, I thought. You just want the days to go by and you want to sleep and forget. Clocks and watches just remind you of upcoming dates with lawyers, judges, and therapists. You long for a world without clocks, a world in which, when you have a happy moment, you can stop the hands on the clock's face from moving and just remain forever and ever imprisoned in that good time.

Dr. Marlowe cleared her throat to remind me I wasn't alone and they were waiting. I sat up again.

"My father," I said, "was a great deal more subtle when it came to my meeting with his attorney. Instead of bringing me to his office for an interview similar to the one I had had with my mother's attorney, he told me he was taking me to lunch the following Saturday.

"My father and my mother belonged to an exclusive country club and often played golf on Saturdays. The entry fee to become a member was very high and that became a contested asset, of course. I thought the whole thing was getting so stupid that it wouldn't surprise me to hear them argue over how many golf balls each owned.

"Anyway, my mother went to play golf with one of her girlfriends and my father took me to lunch at a nice restaurant in Santa Monica where you could sit by a window and look out at the ocean. It wasn't until we were almost there that he informed me his attorney would be joining us.

" 'I just thought this would be a more relaxed setting,' he explained, 'and easier for all of us, not that you should feel uncomfortable with Arnold.'

"Here, I was thinking that at least something good was coming out of all this madness: my father was spending some quality time with me and instead it was another deception. I was sure I could count on the fingers of one hand all the times before when he and I were together alone, doing something that was pure fun.

"I felt this great disappointment, this huge letdown that resembled a kite just falling out of the wind and drifting to earth.

"However, I didn't say anything. There were enough complaints circling my head like moths all day and night. I didn't need to add any.

"We valet parked and went into the restaurant. Arnold was already there waiting at the booth.

" 'My goodness,' he exclaimed as we approached the table, 'look at how tall and beautiful she's become, Michael. I almost didn't recognize her. Hi, Jade.'

" 'Hello,' I said without much feeling and slid into the booth. I looked out at the ocean wistfully, wishing I was outside on that beach, just watching the waves roll in with the wind blowing through my hair. Actually, I was glad we had come here because I could drift off so easily during the dreary conversation.

"Arnold began almost in the same way Mr. Fishman had. He told me how hard he was going to work to make this whole unfortunate event as easy for me as possible. He knew about the custodial assessment, but he put a great deal more emphasis on it than Mr. Fishman had, or I should say, a great deal more pressure on me.

" 'The things you tell this Dr. Morton will have a great impact on the judge,' he said. 'Custodial decisions are usually based on what the judge comes to believe will be in your best interest, not in your mother's or even your father's. The way you describe your relationship with your dad is obviously going to be very important,' he emphasized.

"Arnold's smile was quite different from Mr. Fishman's. Fishman's had been so slick and cold, I could discount it, see through the insincerity instantly. Arnold was harder to read. He had a warmer-looking smile that almost made me think he had my best interests in mind. Almost, but not quite. I soon found out he was just as slimy and self-serving as Mr. Fishman. I suppose they were just two different sides of the same counterfeit coin. It didn't matter which side was up after you flipped it. I was in a phony world of lies.

" 'We don't want you to deal unfairly with your mother,' Arnold continued. 'I know your mother almost as well as I know your father, and I wouldn't want to do anything that wasn't right in regards to her, but what you need to do real soon is think about all the things your father does for you—things we would call day-to-day stuff, like getting you to important places, making sure you get the things you need, being there to talk, stuff like that. You're at the age when a father like yours can be very, very important,' he added with that deceivingly warm smile. 'Especially when you're considering colleges and traveling. Your father's been to an Ivy League school,' he reminded me. 'Your mother hasn't. As I recall, she went to some business school for a year, right Michael?'

" 'The Templeton School of Business. They don't even award an associate's degree,' my father said. I was shocked by the cruelty in his voice—I had never heard him belittle my mother's education like that.

" 'Precisely my point,' Mr. Klugman said. 'Your father's real college experience is what you need to rely on now. You've talked about possible colleges to attend, haven't you?' he asked.

" 'No,' I said.

"Our food had been served but Arnold refused to let me eat in peace.

" 'No?'

" 'No,' I said. 'I had a meeting with my guidance counselor, but both my mother and father were out of town that day even though the meeting had been scheduled a week in advance. The day of the meeting, my mother got called on a company emergency and my father had a very serious problem with one of his big projects. I forget where,' I said dryly. 'My guidance counselor wouldn't cancel on such short notice. I had to have the meeting without my parents.'

"Mr. Klugman turned to my father.

" 'But we went over what you discussed with your guidance counselor. We talked at dinner that night, remember?' my father said.

"I shrugged. To be honest, I couldn't remember if we had or not.

" 'I guess,' I said.

" 'See, that's the sort of thing I want you to try to recall,' Mr. Klugman jumped on. 'You know, it might not be a bad idea to write some of it down. If you have any questions about any of it, ask your dad.'

" 'You make it sound like a final exam or something,' I said.

" 'Oh, it is,' he said. 'It's just like a final exam and much more important.'

"He, too, talked about the other witnesses who would be called and he asked me questions about them.

"I ate fast, more out of nervousness than from

hunger. Afterward, I didn't throw up like I had at my mother's attorney's office, but my food felt like it had all gotten stuck in my throat. I wished I hadn't eaten anything. It actually hurt when I tried to swallow.

"When we started out of the restaurant, I looked longingly at the beach and my father stopped and looked too.

" 'Do you want to take a walk on the beach?' he offered.

"Here he was dressed in a jacket and tie and wearing his expensive Bally shoes. How could we walk on the beach? I wondered.

" 'Yes,' I said and he led me onto the boardwalk.

" 'I'm really sorry about all this,' he began. 'Believe me when I tell you it was the furthest thing from my imagination.'

" 'The divorce or the custody battle?' I asked.

" 'Both,' he replied, 'but I have to admit, your mother surprised me with her decision to go to court about this. I never anticipated which one of us had primary custody was so important to her. I know the house is important, but her freedom to do what she wants to do is clearly what matters the most. At least, that's what I had assumed. Of course, there are other things involved here, more complicated things.'

"I knew what he was saying, but I didn't respond. The hardest thing about all this is to have to deal with each of them when they try to get me to take sides. Why couldn't we just walk on the beach and talk about other things? What about what Mr. Klugman had brought up at lunch: my college future? Neither of my parents had come right out and asked me what I wanted to do with my life. They were both too caught up in what they were doing with their own lives.

" 'I'm not going to lose the house,' he continued. 'My soul is in that house. I created it. It was born right here,' he said pointing to his temple. 'I can claim it as intellectual, artistic property, you know. Arnold is investigating that argument.'

"Here they both were vowing to me that neither would lose the house as if the house was more important than me.

" 'Don't worry,' he assured me. 'Your mother will have something quite upscale as an alternative. She knows that. She's just fighting that battle for spite. You know how much she hates anything that has to do with the house. Can you just imagine her being responsible for maintaining it?'

"He laughed. I kept my eyes down and walked with my arms crossed under my breasts. The ocean breeze felt so cool and refreshing. As we drew closer, I stopped and took off my shoes to walk in the sand. He hesitated, laughed and took off his shoes and socks. He rolled up his pants and joined me as we walked toward the water.

" 'This is fun. I haven't done this in years,' he said.

" 'Maybe that's why there are all these problems,' I muttered.

" 'Oh, is that what she's telling you these days?' he asked, pouncing.

"Jade, I told myself, just keep your mouth shut.

They're both like dynamite sticks with short wicks. Practically every word I said could be a potential spark.

" 'No,' I said. 'You two used to have so much fun together. I just thought that was important.'

" 'It is!' he cried. 'But that old adage is true. It takes two to tango. I could make a list as long as my arm of places, events, things I wanted to do for pure enjoyment that she no longer had the time to do or cared to do,' he explained, which was exactly her complaint about him.

" 'It's all right; it's all right,' he quickly added. 'If that's who she is, if that's who she wants to be, fine. I wish her well, but I need to have a more relaxed relationship. I'm a creative person. I need to avoid stress,' he insisted.

"I stood on the beach and let the tide kiss my toes. He did the same, but rambled on about how things had changed and why he didn't want this to happen and why he hoped she would become reasonable.

"After a while the sound of the sea drowned him out and I closed my eyes and imagined myself on a sailboat, gliding along in the wind, the spray on my face.

" 'We should head back,' I heard him say. 'Jade?'

" 'What? Oh. Yes,' I said and followed him up the beach to a faucet where we could rinse the sand off our feet. He gave me his handkerchief to use as a towel.

"As I wiped my feet, I sensed him standing off to

the side gazing at me, and when I looked at him, I saw this boyish grin on his face. I raised my eyebrows.

" 'What?' I asked with a smile of my own.

" 'Nothing. I was just looking at you and thinking how pretty you are. You look a lot like your mother when she was younger, you know. She's an attractive woman, although,' he said with a small smirk, 'that's never been enough for her. It isn't even a viable compliment. She's ready to claw any man who tells her she's pretty. You're not like that. I know you're not. You're going to be all right, Jade. This will all come to an end and you'll be like a cat and land on your feet, don't worry about that.'

" 'What about you, Daddy?' I asked him.

" 'I'll be fine. *We'll* be fine,' he insisted. He wouldn't consider his future without including me, at least, for now.

"What happens later when either he or my mother win the custody battle? I wondered. Would they both still include me in their lives with such passion?

"I guess what I mean to say is I stopped trusting both of them, trusting what they told me and what they promised."

I gazed at Dr. Marlowe. She nodded softly.

"What I've learned," I continued, "is that once they broke their vows to each other, they lost their credibility with me."

Star was looking at me strangely, as if for the first time she truly understood me. Misty nodded in agreement with me and Cat looked like she was poised to jump up and run from the room. I wondered why what I'd just said had affected her so strongly.

"They lied to each other. Why should I believe them? Ever," I emphasized. "Don't you all feel like that, feel you've been betrayed?"

"I do," Misty agreed.

Cat glanced at Dr. Marlowe and just nodded.

Star smiled softly. "My granny tells me we come into this world without a single guarantee and leave the same way. It's all promises, girl. Take your pick and play your chance."

"Well, I wasn't about to bet on either of them," I said. "I think the therapist making the evaluation has come to that conclusion, too.

"One day soon after I met with Daddy and his attorney, I came home from school and found this woman, Dr. Morton, waiting for me in the living room. Rosina had given her a cold soft drink and she sat with her little clipboard on the settee. As I crossed the hallway, I heard the doctor call my name.

"I paused and looked in at her, curious of course. Dr. Morton is a very short woman, probably an inch shorter than Misty, with very curly, dark brown steel-wool hair, and big almond shaped eyes, beautiful eyes.

"She has a very sincere warm smile. Even if you don't want to be cooperative, you are eventually, and that's because you can see she enjoys her work and sees herself as doing something very critical, almost as critical as heart surgery. She always concentrates on every answer I give her and she looks like she turns all the words around like some diamond cutter, studying, thinking, scrutinizing each syllable. It can almost drive you nuts!" I burst out.

Dr. Marlowe laughed.

"She has a wonderful reputation. Dr. Morton is highly respected," she said.

"I wouldn't want her job," Misty offered.

"It's like King Solomon in the Bible cutting that baby in two," Star said.

"Cutting a baby? I don't remember that," Misty said, "not that I've read much of the Bible."

"He didn't cut it. He said he would when the two women claimed to be the mother. And the one who was the mother told him not to do it. Told him to give the baby to the other woman," Star explained.

"She gave up her child?"

"She'd rather see that happen than the baby dead. That's not so hard to understand."

"My parents would rather see me cut in half," I muttered. Misty spun around to look at me. "I can't help it," I said. "That's how I feel. Stop looking at me like that. I'm not the bad one here."

My stomach tightened again.

"Talk about dynamite sticks," Star said, looking up at me. "No one's accusing you of anything."

"Yeah, maybe not now, but soon, one of my parents will, the one who loses," I said.

"No, they won't," Star said. "Your daddy will just accuse your mother of all that poison you mentioned before, or your mother will do the same to him."

"Maybe," I said, "but I couldn't help being nervous

when I answered Dr. Morton's questions, no matter how harmless she made them sound.

"At first she asked me to talk about myself, my daily routine, my interests, my school work. That moved to what life was like in my house, how often I spent time with my parents, how often I was just with my father or my mother and if I enjoyed spending time with each of my parents. She wanted to know how I felt about either of them not spending more time with me, how interested I was in each of their lives, too. I think she was surprised at how little I know about their work. I wasn't even sure what my mother did at her job, and I couldn't explain what my father was working on at the moment.

"Dr. Morton had a way of keeping her attention on me while she jotted notes. I tried to figure out what was important to her and what wasn't, but everything seemed important. Finally, she asked if she could see my room. I took her upstairs and she walked around, looking at my things. Then she started to ask me questions about dolls, clothes, pictures. Who gave me what? How did I feel about it? What was precious to me? Why? Every time she asked me something and I answered, I couldn't help wondering does that help my father or my mother more?

"Then she set up some 'what if' situations for me and asked for my comments," I said.

"What if's?" Misty asked.

"What if your father won custody but your mother won the house, would you mind moving out with him and living with him someplace else? What if you had to leave the school you were in? What if your mother moved out and wanted you to live in a different part of the city? Would I miss my friends?

"Then she asked how I would feel if the court awarded custody to my father and how would I feel if it awarded custody to my mother?

"She was surprised when I said I didn't care.

" 'Do you say that because you don't want to hurt one or the other?' she asked.

"I thought about it for a moment and said, 'No, I said it because I feel like I'm not living with them now so who I live with afterward won't make much difference.'

"I remember she just stared at me and then jotted something on her clipboard and told me she might be back when my parents were there, too. I told her to call well in advance. 'I don't even know when they'll be here together,' I said.

"I was deeply in it now, deeply in the quicksand their marriage had become, and I hated it more than ever. Because of Rosina, my parents found out that Dr. Morton had been there and each of them found a way to be alone with me to question me about her and the things she wanted to know. Both were surprised I hadn't mentioned her visit myself, and I could see they each took that to mean I might have spoken against them.

" 'What did she want to know about us?' they both asked, but what each really meant was, 'What did she want to know about me and what did you tell her?'

" 'She asked me not to talk about the questions she

asked me,' I told them, 'not that she asked that much or I said much. She had a lot of questions about the house,' I added. Of course, I made that up.

"I know neither was happy with my replies. I felt as if I was living in a spy school or something, each of them peeping around corners now, listening with one ear to my phone conversations, checking my mail, searching for clues as to what I have said and what I would say.

"It got so I didn't want to go home anymore. I dreaded the evenings and especially the dinners if they were both at the table. I could see the way they analyzed my every comment and soon I hardly said a word, or if they asked questions, I kept my answers to one or two words.

"The funeral atmosphere that I had felt in the house before thickened like fog. I could feel the crisis building, the tension stretching until something was bound to snap.

"The only way to escape the awful tension and avoid dealing with either one of them was to lock myself in my room and disappear into the world beyond my computer screen. I'd used my computer mainly for schoolwork but soon I discovered chat rooms where there were people talking about movie stars or bands I liked."

"Chat rooms?" Star asked.

"You don't have a computer?" I thought *everyone* had a computer these days.

"Hardly," she said. "We're lucky we have a microwave."

Misty laughed and even Cat smiled.

"You go on-line and you can talk to people all over the country, all over the world, for that matter."

"Talk?"

"Well, you don't actually talk. You write and they write back instantly and you carry on conversations, sometimes with a dozen people at once. Some of my friends are really into it.

"One night, I noticed a private chat room and just sat back and read the dialogues. Most people make up names to use, but sometimes you can tell a little about them from the names they choose, like Metal Man is probably into heavy rock music, understand?"

"I guess," Star said.

"Anyway, I was reading the conversation and I realized someone named Loneboy had parents who were in a bitter divorce, too. I asked him how old he was and he said seventeen. He said he had a younger brother who was taking the divorce a lot harder than he was. In fact, his little brother was already in therapy because he was acting out, much like you said your brother Rodney was doing, Star, breaking things, getting into fights with other children at school, stuff like that.

"Anyway, Loneboy and I exchanged some information and soon afterward, we skipped the chat room and E-mailed each other directly instead. He told me he lived in San Francisco. The more he told me about himself, the more I told him about myself."

"Why didn't you just call him on the phone?" Star asked.

"I don't know. He didn't suggest it and neither did I. I think he was afraid of hearing my voice or maybe me hearing his. He hadn't told me his name yet. I mean his real name."

"Just Loneboy?" Misty said. "All this time?"

"Yes. I have to admit it was just easier this way. You don't confront the other person as directly. You feel . . . safer," I said looking at Dr. Marlowe.

"I told him most of what I've been telling you. His home situation was a lot stormier, more like Star's in a way. His mother found out his father was seeing another woman and they got into a bad fight in front of the younger brother who saw his father strike his mother. The police were involved. It went from a domestic abuse case to a divorce. Loneboy liked his father but turned on him when he cheated on his mother and they had words. Later, he and his father had a calm conversation and Loneboy said he didn't hate him as much. He understood a little more about his father and why he had cheated on his mother.

"Still, he was unhappy about what was happening to his younger brother and he blamed his father mostly for that because his mother eventually deserted them."

"Why did she desert her own kids?" Misty asked.

"Maybe she just used the marriage problems as an excuse to run off and do what she always wanted to do anyway," Star suggested.

"That's what Loneboy believed, I think, although his father didn't avoid blame. He said he just felt trapped in the bad marriage and didn't know what to do."

"Didn't you ever find out his real name?" Misty asked.

"Finally, he told me his name was Craig Bennet. He gave me his address too and described his home as one that had been in his father's family for a long time."

"And he already knew your name?" Star asked.

"Yes. I didn't know much about chat rooms when I first started going to them so I just used my real name. After a while, Craig started to give me advice about how to deal with my problems at home. Some of it made sense to me, like advising me to get more involved in the things I liked. He said the best thing for me to do at this point was to be self-centered, too, to stop worrying about my parents and their feelings and to care only about my own. Just because they messed up their lives, he said, it didn't mean I had to mess up mine.

" 'Survival,' he said, 'that's what you should think about and how you won't let them ruin your life with their petty problems.'

"He wasn't all seriousness though; he knew lots of good jokes and our Internet relationship grew stronger and stronger until I had the courage to scan my picture and E-mail it to him. I waited nervously to get his response. It came in one word."

"What?" Misty asked.

"Wow!"

Misty laughed.

"I asked him to send me his picture and he did. He wasn't bad-looking, kind of sensitive-looking, in fact. I didn't sent back 'Wow,' but I told him I thought he was a good-looking guy and he shouldn't worry about finding someone.

"He said he already had. Me.

"I began to feel good about myself again, not that I didn't have lots of boys wanting to go out on dates with me, but none of them really wanted to hear about my problems. Craig seemed so much more mature than the boys at school and what I thought I needed at this point in my life more than anything was a mature, good friend, someone who could understand what I was going through. I was really lucky to find someone who was in a situation similar in many ways to my own."

"Yeah, wonderful," Star said. She looked like she was getting bored.

"I'm just trying to explain why I did it," I said.

"Did what?" Star asked.

"Decided that when I ran away, I would run to him. I don't know what I was thinking. I guess I got so desperate for good news and good feelings and thoughts, I let my fantasies explode.

"I envisioned being with someone who understood my every feeling and I wanted to shut the door on my life at home, not answer a single question more, not deal with lawyers or judges, and especially not listen to one of my parents downgrade the other with the hope I would agree.

"One night after the custodial assessment had

begun and statements were being taken from my guidance counselor, some teachers and family friends, my parents had a particularly bad argument. They each accused the other of backstabbing sabotage with the intention of making the other look like an irresponsible parent. Their attorneys had been sniffing around Doctor Morton's assessment to date and apparently she wasn't very complimentary about either of them.

" 'You're trying to get my own daughter to hate me,' my father accused.

" 'That's exactly what you hope to do,' my mother responded. 'Fill her head with lies about me.'

"I slammed my door shut and turned up my music to drown out their voices.

"Later, they each took turns coming to my room to complain about the other. I ignored their complaints and reminded each that it was the week of the Honor Society inductions with a ceremony on Thursday night. I was still a member, somehow keeping my grades up, and there was a reception. Everyone's parents would be there. However, my father had to leave for Texas and my mother had already booked herself in Atlanta for a cosmetics convention. Neither had remembered the affair, but what I understood was when my father knew my mother wasn't going to be there and she knew he wasn't, they were both comfortable with not being there. Know what I mean?"

"Neither would look good to Dr. Morton because they both had deserted you," Cat said.

"That's right."

"But what about you?" Misty asked.

"Yes, what about me?"

They waited.

I smiled.

"I decided I wasn't going to attend either. I had another obligation too."

"What obligation?" Star asked.

"My obligation to run away," I said. "And that was just what I did."

5

"It's probably a good time to break for lunch," Dr. Marlowe said.

"I'd rather hear Jade's story," Misty whined.

"Speak for yourself, girl. My stomach's rumbling and her story will still be here when we get back," Star told her.

"Jade could use the rest, I'm sure," Dr. Marlowe said.

I wasn't hungry, but it was a good idea to stop for a while. When I rose, I felt as if I had been running, not sitting. Riding a roller coaster of emotions, even only in memory, was exhausting.

On a table on the closed-in patio, Emma had set up a buffet of cold cuts, cheeses, some salad, bread and rolls. There was a variety of cookies, too.

"I changed my mind," Misty said when she set eyes on it all, "I'm glad we stopped for lunch."

Star grunted, but Cat actually broke out in a wide smile. I say broke out because for her a smile was something smothered beneath shyness and fear most of the time I had been with her. Whenever she did smile, I felt as if it had escaped from under the weight of sadness that usually soaked her face like ink in a blotter.

"Just dig in, girls," Dr. Marlowe said.

We filled our dishes and sat at the table, Dr. Marlowe joining us last. Emma rushed in and out, replenishing meats and cheeses as if she had three times the number of people for lunch than were actually here.

"Thank you, Emma," Dr. Marlowe called to her as she hurried back to the kitchen.

"Why doesn't Emma eat with us?" Misty asked.

"Maybe she's afraid she'll catch something," Star said.

"What could she catch, a bad attitude?" I said. Star looked at me for a moment and then shook her head and bit into her sandwich.

"Emma has always been very shy," Dr. Marlowe offered. "And she likes to think the best of people, look harder for the good in everyone."

"That's why she's the way she is," Star muttered.

"What do you mean? You don't know how she is," I said. She smirked as if I had said something stupid. "Well, do you?"

"She's living here with her sister like some maid.

What has she got for herself? I'm not blind and I don't look at the world through . . . what did you call them?" she asked Dr. Marlowe. "Rosy-colored glasses?"

"Rose-colored. That's what Emma wears," Dr. Marlowe said, nodding with a smile. "She's not as unhappy as you might imagine, Star. She's comfortable, safe and she's home. She knows I'll do whatever I can for her and she would do the same for me. The way the world seems sometimes, that's a lot."

"Amen to that," Star said, yet I could still see skepticism lurking in her eyes.

After having heard Star's story, I couldn't fault her for doubting Emma's happiness. I just hoped like Dr. Marlowe that we could have a positive effect on each other.

"Do you counsel her too?" Star asked the question we'd all wondered about.

"Not formally, but we talk a lot. You'd be surprised at how much she helps me."

"Were you close when you were younger?" Misty asked.

"Not as much as I would have liked us to be, no," Dr. Marlowe said. "And Emma got married early."

"How early?" Star asked.

"She was just nineteen," Dr. Marlowe said. By now it was possible for me to read her a little and know when something displeased her. I could hear it in her voice and in the way her eyes shifted quickly as if she hoped to change the subject.

"You didn't think she should get married?" I asked, turning the tables on Dr. Marlowe. Let her sit in the hot seat for a while.

"My father was a very strong man, strong-willed. He thought it would be the best thing for her," she said.

"You mean, he arranged it?" Misty asked with those innocent, wide eyes.

"Let's just say he exerted strong influences on everyone concerned," she replied.

"Everybody thinks they know what's best for everyone else," Star chimed in, but looking pointedly at me. "Giving advice at the drop of a moan. There are Dear Abby's preaching on every street corner nowadays."

Dr. Marlowe laughed.

"I'm afraid Star's right about that."

"Maybe people think if they fill their heads with someone else's business, they don't have to worry about their own," Star said.

"You might have something there," Dr. Marlowe told her. "That's an astute comment, Star."

Star took a bite of her sandwich and glittered with glee at the compliment. I couldn't help but laugh.

"What's so funny?"

"Us," I said. "Even thinking for one moment that we have anything to offer anyone else."

"Don't be so hard on yourself, Jade," Dr. Marlowe said. "You'd be surprised how difficulties in life often make you more of an expert than you think. It's why I wanted you all together."

"Maybe she should borrow Emma's glasses," Star said.

Cat laughed so loudly we all turned to her and she blushed.

"You think she's right?" I asked her sharply.

To my surprise she didn't back down. Her eyes looked directly into my own and then she said, "I hope so."

Misty smothered a giggle. Dr. Marlowe's eyes lit like Christmas lights and Star went to the table for seconds.

We'll see how smug and funny they are when they hear the rest of my story, I thought.

And then I asked myself why didn't I want them to be happy?

Was it because misery loves company?

I'd rather be happy and alone.

When we returned to Dr. Marlowe's office I felt like I was coming back to the stage after an intermission, as if I were in a school play. I had been in two plays, one in junior high and one when I was a sophomore and then I stopped trying out even though my drama teacher kept asking me to audition. Maybe I thought if the spotlight hit me, really concentrated on me, everyone in the audience would know I had been turned into a shadow.

Taking a deep breath, I began again.

"I had dinner by myself the night of the Honor Society induction. Mrs. Caron, feeling sorry for me, made my favorite meal: veal cordon bleu."

"What's that?" Star asked, grimacing. "Blue veal?"

"No," I said. "It's veal rolled and stuffed with ham and cheese. It's French."

"Pardon my ignorance," she said. "I'll take my grandmother's fried chicken. That's American."

I raised my eyes toward the ceiling.

"May I continue?" I asked.

"By all means," Star said.

"Thank you. I felt bad for Mrs. Caron, but I really had no appetite. She asked if I was sick and I apologized and told her to save the leftovers for me. She rarely did. My mother has this thing about leftovers. Every week we would throw away enough to feed a family like ours for another week. My father complains a lot about that, but my mother accuses him of wanting to take risks with our health just to save a dollar and he backs down.

"I rose from the table and wandered through the empty house. I could swear the echoes of a hundred recent arguments were bouncing from wall to wall in practically every room. I imagined the house itself taking on a dreariness, the colors fading, the windows clouding as if the storm of my parents' divorce was raining gloom and doom over furniture, pictures, and decorations. Cold hate was dripping down the walls in the house I once thought was my perfect little world.

"It made me laugh to think about that and I guess I laughed so hard and loud, it brought Mrs. Caron and Rosina out of the kitchen to see what was happening.

" 'Are you all right?' Mrs. Caron asked.

" 'What? Oh, yes,' I said. 'I'm fine. I was just laughing at the rain.'

" 'Rain?' She looked at Rosina and they both looked at me with concern. 'It's not raining, Jade.'

" 'No? I guess that's just tears then. The house is crying. Yes, that's it, Mrs. Caron, the house is sobbing. Don't you hear it? Listen,' I said and tilted my head.

"They stared at me with questions in their eyes. I smiled and told them not to worry. My father had designed the house so it could withstand months and months of weeping.

"Then I turned and pounded up the stairway, holding my hands over my ears, and shut myself up in my room. For a while I just sat on the bed and stared at myself in the vanity mirror. I tried to go through the motions of preparing for the Honor Society reception, but after I put on my dress and looked at myself, I just burst into tears.

"It's catching, I told myself. The house is infecting me. I've got to get out of here before it's too late, I told myself. I rushed around my room and threw some clothes together into a small backpack. Then I called for a taxi. First, I had the driver take me to the bank where I withdrew five hundred dollars from the ATM. Then I had him take me to the airport. I bought a ticket to San Francisco on the next flight. I remember looking at my watch during the flight and thinking I would have been sitting on the stage at this moment, gazing out at the audience of parents and friends, looking vainly for my own. I closed my eyes and fell asleep.

"When I arrived in San Francisco, I took a cab to Craig's home. I had no idea what I would say or do when I got there. I just wanted to talk to him, to spend time with him.

"He lived on Richland Avenue near Holly Park. I had been to San Francisco before, but I'd never been to his neighborhood. Craig's house looked as old as he had described it. It was a three-story Italianate with a low-pitched roof. The bottom floor had bay windows and the stucco exterior had faded into a brownish-yellow.

"It was just after nine when I arrived. Most of the windows were dark with just a dull glow in one of the first-floor windows. No one's home, I thought, but went up to the door and rang nevertheless. It took so long for anyone to answer that I had already started back down the short stairway.

" 'Yes?' I heard and turned to see a tall, lean man with thin, graying light brown hair, some of the strands so long, they drooped over his eyes and hung down over his ears. It was hard to make out the details of his face because the light was so dim behind him.

" 'I'm looking for Craig Bennet,' I said nervously.

"He simply stood there, gazing out at me as if I hadn't spoken. For a moment, I wondered if I had only imagined asking for Craig. I repeated Craig's name just in case.

" 'Who are you?' the man asked in return. I told him and again, he just stood there staring.

" 'Oh,' he finally said. 'Craig mentioned you to me. You're the computer girl.'

" 'Yes,' I said, smiling at the label. 'I'm the computer girl.'

"The way I was feeling, I might as well have been something created in a computer.

" 'Well, what are you doing here?' he asked.

" 'I came to San Francisco and I thought it would be nice for us to finally meet face to face,' I said.

" 'Oh sure. That is nice. Come on in,' he said.

" 'Is Craig at home?' I asked, hesitating. My legs were smarter than my brain. They held back on their own.

"No, not at the moment. He's gone on some errands for us, but he'll be home very soon,' he said.

"He stepped back and waited, holding the door open for me.

" 'Come on in. He won't be long,' he promised.

"I walked up the steps and entered the house. It was so dark and musty. There was a lot of wood trim along the entryway and on my right was a grandfather clock that wasn't working.

" 'I was just reading,' he said. 'You kids don't do enough of that these days, not since you discovered computers. Come into the living room. Can I get you something to drink?'

" 'No thank you,' I said, following him. The living room was small and cluttered with antique furniture."

"How did you know so much about all that?" Star asked skeptically. It was as though she thought I was making up the whole thing. As if I would make up something like this.

"My father," I said. "Some of it rubbed off whether I wanted it to or not.

"Getting back to what I was saying," I added, "he had one lamp on by a threadbare Chippendale wing chair." I said it with deliberate exactness to annoy her now.

" 'Well, have a seat,' he offered, indicating the settee across from him. 'You look like you just arrived in town.'

" 'I did,' I said.

" 'Who you visiting with?'

" 'No one,' I made the mistake of saying. 'I mean, it's a spur of the moment trip.'

"He smiled and sat. Under the lights I could see the resemblances between him and Craig from the picture Craig had attached to his E-mail. His eyes were as deeply set and his nose the same nearly perfectly straight shape, just a trifle too long, but adding character. His mouth had similarly full masculine lips and he had the same soft curve from his cheekbone to his jaw.

" 'Craig's quite taken with you,' he said. 'He talks about you a lot.'

" 'Does he? We did sort of hit it off and I thought it would be great to finally meet.'

"There was a strange smell—more than just a musty odor now. It smelled more like incense or something. I guess I twitched my nose and he saw it and laughed.

" 'We just finished dinner a little while ago. I'm not the best cook. I burned the potatoes. We were about to have coffee when we discovered we didn't have any. We're both failing pretty bad at domestic chores,' he explained. There was a little lisp in his speech and from the way his mouth dipped on the right side when he spoke, I wondered if he hadn't suffered a stroke or something. Now that I looked at him more closely, I could see how thin he was and how his right shoulder slanted a bit lower than his left.

" 'Where's Sonny?' I asked, referring to Craig's younger brother.

" 'Oh, he went along with him. You can't keep those two apart. Nothing Sonny likes more than spending time with Craig. He looks up to him like Craig's a superhero, and Craig loves and protects him. They've come together like this,' he said, holding his hand up in a tightly closed fist. 'Since she left us, all three of us are like this.'

" 'That's nice,' I said smiling. It did sound nice, although from some of the things Craig had said in his E-mails, I didn't think life was as rosy as Mr. Bennet portrayed.

" 'He told you about this house?' he asked.

" 'Yes,' I said.

" 'You can appreciate it since your father's an architect, I bet. It was something in its day.'

" 'Craig really has told you a lot about me, I see,' I said. 'You know my father is an architect.'

" 'Oh, yes. We don't keep much from each other anymore. That's because we're all like one,' he said, holding up that bony fist again. 'She didn't destroy us when she ran off. She made us stronger. In some ways I'm glad she went. She was never happy being tied down. She had the wanderlust. We got married too early. It was as if I had tamed a wild horse or something. Babies were lead weights around her neck. She and I stopped making love after Sonny was born; she was afraid of having another child. You know what happens to a marriage once the romance goes out of it?'

" 'Yes,' I said and thought it was a strange conversation for him to have with a total stranger, but I imagined that in his mind, because of my E-mail correspondence with Craig, he didn't think of me as a complete stranger.

" 'Craig told you a little about the divorce, right?' he asked. 'I know you told him all about your parents' situation.'

" 'Yes.' I said.

"Actually, I was getting a little upset at how much Craig had told his father. None of my friends would have shared so much with their parents. Had Craig gone so far as to print out my letters? I wondered.

"As if he could read my thoughts, Mr. Bennet added, 'Craig often read your letters at dinner to us. I'm sorry for your troubles at home. Your parents sound like . . . dummies,' he suggested. 'Why can't they see what they're doing to you? It pains Craig to read some of that stuff. He gets so angry, he can't eat. He wants to know why adults are so cruel to their own children.

" 'Then he starts talking about his own mother and asking me more questions so he can tell you about her, I think. I hate talking about her. I try to forget her. I even got so I can't recall her face anymore. You can push things out of your mind if you want to, you know. You just think of something else every time the bad things come up. You say, no, no to it. Get out, out!' he practically screamed.

" 'I used to sit in front of a mirror and stare into my own eyes and just dare a memory to come into my head. You should try it sometime. It helps, believe me,' he said.

"I smiled at him and gazed around curiously. The room looked like it needed more than just a good dusting. I saw cobwebs in the corners and layers of dust on the marble mantel. When I gazed down at the floor around his chair, I saw what looked like caked old food and I could have sworn I caught sight of a rat slipping behind the armoire."

"Ugh," Misty cried. "Why didn't you just leave?"

"I still wanted to see Craig.

" 'You're as pretty as your picture,' Mr. Bennet said. 'Craig's going to be happy you came. I know what,' he said, slapping his hands together, 'why don't I show you his room and his computer while you wait?'

" 'He might not like that,' I said.

" 'Sure he will. Don't you want to see it? That's where your friendship began. It's like . . . like something historic for you two. Right?'

" 'Yes, but . . .'

" 'Well, then don't be shy. Not with Craig. Not after all you two have shared. Why, he's told you more about us than he's told relatives and best friends, and I bet you've done the same. I can see from the look on your face that you have. That's nice. That's something unusual these days . . . trust. You're the nicest thing to come into his life since . . . since before,' he said, and I could tell he was doing what he described: keeping the bad memories out.

" 'I bet you'd like to see this old house anyway,' he added, standing up. 'He told you how long it's been in the family, right?'

" 'Yes,' I said. 'I know the style. My father built a house like this for a client in Beverly Hills two years ago.'

" 'This house was built in 1870,' he began proudly as he headed for the door. He paused, waiting. Once again, my smarter legs hesitated, but I forced myself up and followed him out. 'Of course, a lot was done to it since, but not so much over the past forty years or so.

" 'Craig's room is on the third floor with the best view,' he said, leading me up the rickety stairway after he flipped a switch that lit up a small, naked bulb overhead.

"We wound around and up. The second-floor landing was narrow and smaller than I had anticipated and the third floor was really more like an attic. There was just one bedroom and an adjoining small bathroom. He turned on the light and I saw the computer on the desk to the left. It was on, the monitor glowing. In the center of the room was a four-poster bed, and to the right of that, a dresser and a closet. The bed was neatly made, almost as tightly tucked as a military bunk.

"There was little on the walls, some pictures of Craig and Sonny but when they were considerably younger, a picture of a jet plane and a poster of an old Star Trek movie. It gave me a strange feeling, like I was moving back through time rather than looking in on what was someone's present bedroom.

" 'Here,' Mr. Bennet said, 'look at this.' He was at the computer table. 'Your most recent letter.' He held it up and I walked in and looked at it. It was my most recent E-mail. 'Just take a gander at that view from that window,' he suggested, moving away from the computer. 'You'll see why Craig would rather stay up here than any other part of this house. We've still got one of the best views in the neighborhood. Go on,' he urged.

"I walked to the window and looked out. The casing was so caked with dust, it was obvious that the window hadn't been opened for a long time, maybe even years. The view was nice, especially because it was night and there were so many lights.

" 'Very nice,' I said, turning. He was at the door, smiling.

" 'Good. I'm glad you like it. Enjoy,' he said and stepped out into the hall. 'I'll tell Craig you're up here when he comes home.'

" 'What?' I gasped as he closed the door. 'Wait,' I cried. I moved toward it but stopped when I heard the lock click. It was one of those skeleton key door locks that you could shut from the outside. The click was like a bullet whizzing by my head. What was going on? I wondered.

"I ran to the door and pulled on the handle, shocked now that he had locked me in.

" 'Mr. Bennet!' I cried. 'What are you doing? Why did you lock the door? Let me out. Please.'

"I could hear his footsteps as he descended the stairway and then all was silent and the glow of the computer played shadows on the opposite wall. I pounded on the door and screamed and pounded and then listened, but I heard nothing. I put my ear against the door, pounded and waited and listened and then I heard some music start below, light, big band music.

"I returned to the window, thinking I might be able to open it and shout down to someone on the street, but the casing really was as good as welded shut. For a few moments I toyed with the idea of smashing the window."

"That's what I would have done," Star said.

"Me too," Misty agreed.

Cat had her head down, her arms embracing herself. She looked like she was trembling. That's what I was like in that room, I thought.

"I thought about it, but to be honest, I was afraid of what he might do to me if I broke his window."

"You were worrying about his window?" Star asked, incredulous.

"Not his window. She was worried about what he'd do to *her,*" Misty piped up. "Obviously, the man was deranged to have locked her in. You don't just challenge such people."

"What are you, an expert?" Star fired back at her.

Misty shrugged.

"She's right," I said, "and besides, I was hoping that Craig would be back any moment like Mr. Bennet had said and would come up and rescue me," I added before they could continue their argument.

"Sure. A crazy man locks you in a room and you decide to wait around. That makes a lot of sense," Star muttered and shook her head.

"While I waited, I explored the room," I continued. "I opened the dresser drawers. They were all empty. I looked in the closet and saw only half a dozen naked hangers. In the corner on the floor was some sort of rodent nest."

"Oh my God," Misty moaned. "You mean, rats?"

"Ugh," Star said.

"Anyway," I said, "I closed the door and went to the computer. There were some notes scribbled on a pad beside it. They looked like E-mail addresses. Mine was included.

"I tried the door again, pulling on it, pounding and then I sat on the bed, trying to think what I should do next. Where was Craig? Was he even coming home? I wondered. Moments later, I heard footsteps on the stairway. They sounded like someone running up and I assumed it was Craig, angry about what his father had done. I heard him stop just outside the door. I waited and listened, but all I heard was the music from below. Then I saw the door knob turning, but the door didn't open.

" 'Craig?' I called. 'Is that you?'

" 'Yes,' I heard after a long moment of silence. His voice was higher pitched than I had imagined it would be. 'I'm sorry about this. He's not well. The son has become the father in this house.'

" 'Can you open the door?' I asked calmly. This was something he had never mentioned in his letters to me, you see.

" 'I thought he left the key in the lock,' he said. 'I have to go back down and get it from him. I'll be right back,' he said.

"I heard his footsteps on the stairs descending quickly. What a mess I put myself in, I thought and tried to remain calm and keep my heart from thumping like a bongo drum. For a minute or two, all I heard was the music. Then, I heard loud voices, clearly voices in argument. I thought I even heard something smash against the wall, then more arguing and then silence. Even the music stopped. I waited by the door, listening hard for footsteps on the stairs.

"They came, but very slowly, heavy. At one point they paused and I called out. They started again and finally they reached the third-story landing. I stepped back from the door and waited.

"I heard the key in the lock. My heart wasn't thumping anymore. It was more like an oil drill pounding deeper and deeper until it vibrated down my spine. The back of my neck was perspiring so much, strands of my hair were soaked.

"The door opened slowly and Mr. Bennet was standing there. My heart sunk. What had he done to Craig? What would he do to me?

" 'I'm sorry,' he said in that high-pitched voice. 'My father is not the same since she left. There's no telling what he'll do sometimes. I didn't write about it in my E-mail because I never thought you'd come here like this, but I'm glad you did,' he added.

"I just stared, my eyes probably close to popping."

"How weird," Misty said in a loud whisper. She had her hands pressed to the base of her throat. Cat was biting down on her lower lip and even Star looked absolutely terrified. Dr. Marlowe sat watching them, her eyes moving slowly from one to the other and then back to me.

" 'You're not Craig,' I managed to say.

"He laughed.

" 'Oh, that was an old picture I sent. It's me, in the flesh, your old computer sidekick, Loneboy.'

"I shook my head, tried to swallow and then took a deep breath so I could speak.

" 'I made a mistake,' I said. I tried to smile, tried not to show my absolute terror. 'I have to go.'

" 'Oh, but you just arrived as I understand it. Don't go just yet. We have a lot to talk about. You want something to eat, drink?'

" 'No thank you,' I said, edging toward the door.

However, he kept himself smack in front of it, blocking it.

" 'Go sit on my bed. It's comfortable,' he urged, nodding toward the bed. 'Go on.'

" 'I'd rather we went downstairs. The living room was nice,' I said.

" 'Naw. He won't let us talk. He'll butt in and Sonny will want us to pay him attention. We're better off staying up here. Go on. Sit,' he ordered.

"I shook my head.

" 'I really have to go,' I said.

" 'Oh, you can't leave now,' he pleaded. 'You're the first girl I've had up here, ever. I've dreamed of it, but you're the first. C'mon. Sit,' he repeated, moving toward me.

"I jumped back, holding my backpack up in front of me like a shield now.

"He smiled.

" 'Oh, you brought stuff. That means you're staying for a while. Good,' he said.

" 'No,' I cried. 'I've got people waiting for me. They're expecting me and will come looking for me.'

"His smile faded. It seemed to sink into his face.

" 'I thought you came to San Francisco to see me,' he said.

" 'I did, but I can't stay. I'm late,' I said, edging around, hoping to squeeze by him.

" 'You want to leave me, too,' he suddenly declared, as though he had come to some realization and it filled his eyes with anger. 'Just like her, you want to leave. You tell me you love me and you care and then you leave. That's cruel. That's selfish. Why don't you care about me? Was all that stuff you wrote just garbage? Why don't you mean what you say?'

" 'I do,' I said quickly. 'That's why I showed up. You were the first person I thought about when I decided to come here,' I added.

His smile returned.

" 'I'm glad.'

" 'But I have to meet some people, relatives.'

" 'You never mentioned having any relatives here,' he said suspiciously.

" 'I know. I had forgotten about them. They called and invited me and I came, but I told them I had to stop by and say hello to you first,' I added. I was thinking as fast as I could, heaving words and thoughts at him in the hope that he would be satisfied and step aside.

"He didn't move.

" 'I'll be back tomorrow,' I promised. 'We'll spend the whole day together.'

" 'No, you won't,' he said, shaking his head. 'That's what she said before she left us. She said, I'm just going away for a little while. Don't be sad. I'll be back soon. I believed her and I waited. Every night, I sat by the window and looked out at the street and waited, but she didn't return. She just said she would.'

" 'But I will,' I insisted. 'I'm not her. I'm Jade, remember?'

"He didn't look like he was listening to me anymore. His eyes were glassy and he seemed to be gazing through me at his memories now. He seemed frozen, almost catatonic, so I started toward the door, inching along. Then, I lunged for it and he reached around and seized my hair, tugging me back with such force, I fell to the floor.

"I screamed and screamed and he just stood there looking down at me as if I was some curious new creature. He wasn't bothered or afraid or even angry. He was just looking at me until my throat ached and I stopped, covering my face as I began to sob.

"He reached down slowly and first took my backpack out of my hands. He tossed it out the door. Then, he surprised me by seizing the backs of both of my feet and pulling my shoes off. He tossed them out the door, too."

"Why?" Misty asked, grimacing.

"He didn't want her to leave," Cat said. It was as if her voice came out of nowhere, as if she was a ghost that had come to life.

Everyone turned to her and she looked down and then back up at me.

"Then what did he do?" Star asked.

"I don't know if I want to hear it," Misty moaned.

"I pushed myself back on the floor and he continued to hover over me.

" 'Go ahead and sit on the bed,' he said calmly. 'It's comfortable.'

"He took another step toward me and I did as he asked.

" 'Now isn't that better than the floor?' he asked.

" 'If you don't let me leave, you're going to be in big trouble,' I told him.

" 'If you leave, you won't come back,' he said. 'You'll run out on us, on me and Sonny. It's not our fault what he did to you. Why do you want to run out on us?'

" 'You're confused,' I said. 'Please, let me go.'

"My stomach felt so hollow. My whole body was shaking. I wanted to fight him, but I was terrified that I would be too weak and he might hurt me very badly.

"He reached back and closed the door behind him. Then he smiled at me.

" 'I'm glad you came back,' he said. 'We have so much to talk about, so much to catch up on.'

"He started toward me and I shook my head, hoping I could make it all disappear. He put his hand on my head and stroked my hair and then held my head in his hands and leaned over to kiss the top of my head."

"You should have kicked him where he'd remember it forever," Star said.

"I thought about it for a second. My heart was racing. I could barely breathe. When he put his hands on my shoulders, I tried to push his arms away and I did try to kick up, but he pressed harder and harder. I was surprised at how strong his fingers were. They seemed to cut through my jacket, through my blouse and into my skin.

"Maybe he cut off the blood to my head. I don't

know, but one moment I was trying to struggle and looking up at him and the next . . ."

"What?" Misty asked, gasping. She had reached across the sofa to Cat and found her hand. Cat let her hold on, or maybe Cat was holding on to her.

"I passed out," I said.

"And when I woke up, I was on my back on the bed, naked."

6

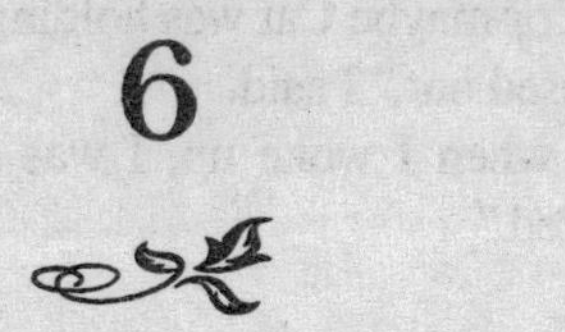

All the girls looked sick to their stomachs. Misty's face was pale, Star's mouth gaped open and Cat had to be excused to go to the bathroom.

"Let me check on her," Dr. Marlowe said, rising. "Everybody take a deep breath. Maybe step outside and get some air, if you want," she added.

We watched her go, nobody moving.

"Do you want to go outside?" Star asked me. I nodded.

We rose and went to the patio door, stepping into the afternoon sun. It felt good on my face, almost like a mother's kiss should feel when she wants to reassure you.

"You sure don't look like a girl who had all that happen to her," Star said warmly. "Granny's always saying don't judge a book by its cover. Turn a few pages first and look it over and then she always adds, 'Remember, he without sin cast the first stone.' She's always telling me stuff like that. She's trying to make up for all the Sunday school and church I missed, I guess."

An awkward silence fell between us. Misty still looked shaken by my story and my own mind was back in that room in San Francisco.

"What's with that Cat girl? Do you think she'll talk tomorrow?" Star asked, finally breaking the tension.

"After what she's heard from us, she's probably going to be on her way out of the country," Misty said.

We all laughed. I saw Star staring at me.

"What?"

"Nothing," she said.

I smiled at her.

"It's all right. We're all going to be all right," I said.

"Another pair of rose-colored glasses working away," she declared.

Misty and I laughed and then we heard Dr. Marlowe returning with Cat. I looked through the patio door and watched Cat sit and Dr. Marlowe leaning over her, offering some comforting words.

"Maybe I'm not doing her any good," I thought aloud.

"Dr. Marlowe wouldn't let you talk if she thought that, would she?" Misty asked. "I mean, she knew most of what you're telling us, right?"

"Most," I said. "But not all," I admitted. "More seems to come back to me than usually does when I'm alone with her, but there's still a lot left to tell."

"I guess that's why she wanted us to do this," Star said. "The same was true for me."

"Me too," Misty said.

I nodded.

Dr. Marlowe took her seat and looked out at us.

"Time to go back," I said. I took a deep breath as if I was going under water. "Let's get it over with."

We returned to the office and our seats.

"How are you doing, Jade?" Dr. Marlowe asked.

"I'm all right."

"We could stop and let you continue tomorrow."

"No, I don't want to sleep on any of it," I said and she nodded, smiling in understanding.

I turned to the girls.

"He didn't rape me," I said quickly. "When I was unconscious, I dreamed of someone's lips on my cheek, in my hair, then lightly over my eyelids and finally on my lips, but nothing more had happened. Star was right. Everything he did, he did mostly to keep me from leaving. In his madness he figured that if I didn't have clothes, I wouldn't try to escape."

Cat looked like I had taken a weight off her shoulders, as if what had happened to me could have happened to her.

"When you realized what he had done, did you break the window?" Misty asked.

"I couldn't reach it," I said.

"What? Why not?" Misty followed. Star nodded like she already knew.

"He had tied my left ankle to the bed and my right wrist. He used the computer cables—I guess he didn't want me to be able to call for help over the Internet. If only I'd thought of that sooner. Turn and twist as much as I could, I was unable to reach the knots and the movement cut through my skin. My ankle actually started to bleed."

"Oh no," Misty cried. "What happened next?"

"I lay there as quietly as I could, trying to keep from passing out again. I was terrified of what he might do next.

"It seemed like hours before he returned. He entered the room, smiling. He was carrying a children's book in his hand.

" 'Oh, you're still awake,' he said. 'I bet you've been having those nightmares again. Don't worry. I'll help you fall asleep.'

" 'Please,' I pleaded. 'Cut me loose. It's hurting me.'

" 'No, no,' he assured me. 'Nothing will hurt you now. You're safe, forever and ever with me.'

"The sound of that put the greatest terror in me. It occurred to me that my parents would never be able to discover where I had gone. They might, with the help of the police, find out I had bought a plane ticket to San Francisco, but I had never told them about Craig and our E-mail relationship. It might take months, maybe years before a smart detective might look in my computer for leads.

"I started to cry. I couldn't help it. He smiled as if that was good and pulled the computer chair beside the bed. Then he wiped the tears from my cheeks and actually tasted them."

"What?" Star asked. "Did you say, tasted?"

"Yes. He nodded and smiled and said, 'I love the salty taste of your tears. I know sometimes you cry just to make me happy.'

"He looked so contented. I forced myself to stop crying. Then he sat back, opened the book and began reading a story meant for a preschooler. He read it to me as if I were only three or four years old, exaggerating everything, raising and lowering his voice, acting happy and then sad when it was appropriate. I didn't utter a sound. When he finished, he closed the book and then leaned over and kissed my cheek.

" 'Time to sleep,' he said.

" 'Please,' I begged, 'let me go.'

" 'I'll stay with you until you fall asleep,' he promised and then, he lowered his head to my stomach and rested it there.

" 'I hear you gurgling,' he said and laughed. 'Go to sleep stomach. Go to sleep kidneys and liver, spleen and gall bladder. You, too, heart. C'mon now,' he said, touching me. I cringed, but he didn't do any more. I could feel his hot breath on my skin. I was as still as I could be and soon his breathing was so regular, I was sure he was asleep."

"On your stomach?" Misty asked.

"Yes. Now I was afraid to move too fast or hard, afraid to wake him. All I could do was close my eyes and try to do what he had said he did all the time, drive out the bad thoughts. I thought about my house, my bedroom, my comfortable bed and I pretended I was home, pretended I had never run away. Exhausted from all the fear and the struggle, I did fall asleep.

"I woke sometime in the middle of the night. I was still tied down, of course, but I managed to turn my body in very slow moves, enduring the pain until I was able to touch the cable with my free hand. I traced it down and worked on tugging it away from my skin. It took hours and hours to gain a quarter of an inch of space, but that was not yet enough.

"It was exhausting, too. I fell asleep again and then I was awakened by the sound of the key in the door. It was morning, but very early because it looked like the sun had just risen. He entered the room, carrying a tray of breakfast: a glass of orange juice, some toast, a bowl of cornflakes with bananas and a flowery weed.

" 'I picked this for you this morning,' he said. 'Isn't it pretty?'

"I was still very afraid, but also very angry now.

" 'You've got to eat your breakfast,' he said. 'It's the most important meal of the day.'

" 'How can I eat? I can't even sit up,' I said.

"He looked at my tied ankle, thought for a moment and then put the tray on the chair. He untied my ankle.

" 'You can eat with one hand,' he said. Even in his madness, he had some logic. He wasn't stupid.

"At this point, I thought it was best to play along so

I nodded, pulled my legs up and let him put the tray on my lap.

" 'That's freshly squeezed orange juice,' he said. 'Nothing but the best for you. Go on, drink it.' "

"It could have been poison," Misty said.

"I thought of that, but I didn't know what else to do but sip it. It tasted good. Then I smiled and said, 'Please, I have to go to the bathroom.'

" 'That's all right,' he said. He went out to the bathroom and returned with a bedpan."

"You mean like in a hospital?" Misty asked.

"Exactly. I shook my head and said, 'Please, I want to go into the bathroom.'

" 'Oh no,' he said, 'you can't get out of bed yet. You're not well enough.' He slipped the bedpan under me. Then he sat watching as if I was some kind of a toy."

"I feel like I'm going to puke," Misty said.

"What do you think she felt like?" Star shot at her.

Cat just stared ahead, waiting.

"I couldn't help it. I had to pee. He left with the bedpan. I can't tell you how weak and sick I felt.

" 'Finish your breakfast,' he said from the doorway. 'I'll be back a little later. I have a few chores. I'm going to make us a great dinner tonight, and I promise,' he said smiling, 'I won't burn anything.'

"Then he closed the door, locked it and descended. I waited for a while before putting the tray on the chair. With more room now because my foot was free, I worked harder and harder on the cable around my other wrist. I got myself enough space to turn my body and step off the bed. Then I saw where the cable was tied to the bed and was able to get it untied. It seemed to take hours and I kept stopping to listen for him. Sure enough, I heard him returning so I fixed the cable loosely and then I got back onto the bed. I dumped the cereal behind the bed and shoved the toast under the pillow just as he worked the key in the lock.

"It must have grown very cloudy and overcast because the room was so dark now and when I gazed out, it looked like it was going to storm. It made me feel even more frightened and cold.

" 'Well, well,' he said, 'you ate everything. Good.' He took the tray off the bed and then he pulled my ankle back down so he could retie it.

" 'Look what I brought you,' he said and gave me another children's book. 'I'll be back later to read it to you, but you can look at all the pictures now.'

"He gazed down at me happily. 'It's so good to have you back,' he said. 'So good.' He touched my forehead and then he turned and left, locking the door again.

"I waited for the silence and then I rose and undid the cable that held my wrist. It took longer to free my ankle, but finally, I was able to move about the room freely."

"But you were still locked in," Misty reminded me and everyone else.

"Exactly.

"Again, I didn't just break the window and scream. What if I was unable to attract anyone's attention? I was afraid he'd hear me and come back to the room in a rage. For a few minutes, I just looked frantically about the room, searching for some idea, some means of escape and then I got down and looked under the bed. You can imagine the balls of dust, but I saw a bedspring was broken and I worked it loose.

"Then I straightened it out as best I could and went to the keyhole. It took forever. I nearly gave up a few times, but finally I heard the lock click. I tried the knob and the door opened. I returned to the bed and pulled off the sheet to wrap around me before returning to the doorway.

"I stood there, trembling, afraid to step out for fear he would be waiting in the small hallway. Cautiously, I peered around and saw there was no one. I also spotted my backpack and my shoes against the wall.

"As quickly as I could, I pulled out a pair of panties, jeans and a blouse. I put on socks and my shoes. I don't think I ever dressed as fast.

"Now that I was dressed and considering my escape, I was even more afraid. Just gazing down that dimly lit stairway put a finger of ice on the back of my neck, a finger that traced down my spine and made me shudder.

"I began to descend. The first step groaned, so loudly I thought, there was no way he wouldn't hear and there wasn't any other way out of the house from this level as far as I could see."

"No fire escape?" Star asked.

"Maybe there was, but I didn't think of it. I kept going down the stairs, each step creaking louder than the one before it, and no matter how slowly I went and how nimbly I stepped, the stairway croaked like some giant frog. It was as if the house was being loyal to its owner and was trying to warn him about my escape. Even the railing rattled. I debated whether I should just charge down the stairs as fast as I could or continue to sneak along. I decided to risk taking my time.

"When I reached the second floor, I paused and listened. He could easily be in any of the rooms, I thought. I heard nothing now, not even the music I had heard the night before. The whole house continued to creak and moan as the wind outside stirred up and whirled about it.

"Just above me the dim light flickered. The rain had started and I could hear the pitter-patter of drops on the roof and against the windows. Shadows along the vaguely lit walls seemed to tremble like ghosts suffering a sympathetic chill. My imagination was like some caged animal, flailing about and coming up with so many crazy and frightening thoughts and images. I had the kind of rippling sensation on the back of my neck you get when you feel someone is watching you. I searched every shadow, every doorway, looking for eyes. Was someone else in this house?

"My heart thumped. I couldn't swallow and it felt like a heavy weight on my chest, but I went on. I don't know where I found the strength to continue moving forward, but I did.

"When I reached the bottom floor, I stopped, caught my breath and listened. It was so quiet, I considered that he might have gone out again. Practically tiptoeing now, I started for the front door and paused when I heard what sounded like a little boy whimpering.

"It continued for a few more moments and then stopped. I realized it was coming from the living room, dead ahead of me and between me and the front door. I could barely keep myself from releasing a sob or a cry of fear. I felt like I was squeezing the breath back into my lungs. I know I was fighting hysteria, pushing my fears down long enough to get strength to go forward.

"As I reached the living room door, I peered through and saw him in his chair. He had my clothes crushed in his arms and against his body like he was embracing a child and he was asleep, his head thrown back and his mouth quivering with nightmare sobs.

"I stepped up to the door and tried to open it as quietly as I could, only it was locked the same way my room upstairs had been locked, with an old-fashioned skeleton key. My heart sank.

"I turned and headed back into the house, hoping that he hadn't locked a rear or side door. All the lights were off and the storm made it so dark inside, I was terrified of knocking into something and waking him. I practically glided down the hallway to the kitchen where I saw another door, but it was locked as well."

"You should have brought that bedspring down with you and used it again," Misty said.

"Yeah, I thought of that, but going upstairs to get it was not an option in my mind."

"Wouldn't have been in mine either," Star said.

"I looked over the countertop carefully, hoping maybe I would find a key, but there wasn't any. Finally I found a window that would open and I raised it a jerky inch at a time. It went about six inches before it got so stuck I couldn't move it. I groaned and strained until I was exhausted. I just wanted to sit down and cry. A throbbing pain in my head stabbed sharply. What had I gotten myself into?"

"How were you supposed to know a weirdo was writing you those E-mails?" Star asked quickly. I smiled at how she didn't want me to blame myself, but I knew it was my own doing. I should have been more careful and not thrown myself into a stranger's world.

"I tried another window and it was worse. How did he ever get fresh air? I wondered. This house was like a dungeon in which all the terrible memories were being held prisoner inside that sick man, I thought."

"So what did you do?" Misty asked. "How did you finally get out?"

"I didn't want to wander around the house looking for a window that would open. I was sure I would knock something over or do something to call his attention to me, so I took a chance and returned to the front door. He was still asleep in the living room.

"I looked around, saw that the space between the wall and the grandfather clock was wide enough to hide me, and then I pounded on the front door and hurriedly hid behind the grandfather clock. I waited and waited, my heart ticking as loud as that clock once ticked, I imagine. He didn't come. After a good minute, I tiptoed over to the door and looked in on him. He had turned, but hadn't awakened, so I returned to the front door and pounded harder and longer. I hit it so hard, I thought the house shook. Desperation gave me the needed strength. Then I hurried behind the grandfather clock again and this time, I heard him stumble around and come out mumbling.

" 'Who's there?' he called. He listened and then he went to the door and listened. 'Little bastards,' he muttered, I guess thinking some neighborhood kids were playing a joke on him. Maybe they had done that before. He did what I hoped he would. He took the key from his pocket and unlocked the door. It was my intention to just rush out, knock past him and lunge out of the house, screaming for help, but he paused and turned to look toward the stairway. I could see he was thinking hard. He closed the door and started for the stairs, only he hadn't locked the door again. My plan had worked.

"I waited until he started up and had time to make the first turn before I stepped out, opened the door and flew down that small stairway to the street. When I got there, I ran and ran, not knowing where I was heading, ignoring the sheets of rain that were whipping at me. I just wanted to get as far away as I could. I ran until I was out of breath and a stitch in my side made me stop. I stood against a fence, holding my side and catching my breath. I was literally soaked, my hair drenched, the water running down my face, but I didn't care. I was so happy, I didn't feel anything else.

"Then I walked down to the far corner, crossed the street and walked until I spotted a restaurant. I went inside to the bathroom and dried myself as best I could. Then I called for a taxi to take me back to the airport. When I got there, I had to wait another hour for a flight back to Los Angeles.

"I nearly fell asleep and missed it. I did fall asleep when I got on the plane. I remember thinking, so much for my running away from home to see someone who could sympathize with me.

"There wasn't any place I could run to, I thought. That's all I had learned on this trip."

"That wasn't all," Star said.

"No, I guess not." I looked at Dr. Marlowe. "I guess I learned a lot about trust.

"Anyway, it was quite late in the day by the time I arrived at my house. Of course, my parents were still away and there was no one checking up on me. Occasionally, Mrs. Caron would look in on me or ask how I was when they were both away, but that was the extent of it. I entered the house very quietly. There was no one waiting around to greet me. When I checked my answering machine, I found a message from my girlfriend Sophie. She wanted to know why I hadn't attended the Honor Society induction ceremony and reception. She told me it was the nicest one."

"People always do that, even your supposed best friends. They tell you something was great when you miss it," Star muttered.

I laughed. It was as if she had known Sophie as long as I had.

"There were no other messages. Apparently neither of my parents had called. You can imagine how exhausted I was. I practically passed out before my head hit the pillow. I slept right through breakfast the following day. I vaguely heard Mrs. Caron outside my door asking if I was feeling all right. It took my missing two breakfasts before she would bother inquiring. I couldn't blame her. I was never one to appreciate her concern and she had decided early on that she would do her work and not poke her nose into our lives.

"I shouted that I was fine and thanked her for asking. She went away without asking any other questions.

"About an hour later, I showered, dressed, had a bagel and some coffee and went to school. I was in quite a daze most of the day. All the rest of the day, people asked why I hadn't attended the Honor Society function and I just used a stomachache as an excuse.

"My mother was the first to return home late in the afternoon. She flew by my room, saw I was sprawled on my bed, and came back.

" 'Hi,' she said. 'I'm having a maddening time. Felix lost the orders for the entire Longs Drugs account. Can you imagine? His computer crashed. You can't imagine what's going on, and all this while I was away.

" 'Oh, how was the Honor Society function?' she asked without pausing for a breath.

"I just stared at her. If I hadn't been lucky, I might be dead up in a room in a strange house in San Francisco, I thought, and my mother had no idea, not in her wildest imaginings, what I had been through. Orders for lipstick and make-up products were temporarily missing and her world was in turmoil. For a moment I wished I was a tube of mascara."

Misty laughed and Star and Cat smiled.

" 'I didn't go,' I told her.

" 'Oh. Why not?'

" 'I wasn't feeling well,' I said. I wanted to blurt, I ran away from home two days ago, used some of my special funds designed to make me independent and confident, and searched for a soul mate who didn't exist. Instead, Mom, some crazed man tried to keep me prisoner. He even took off my clothes after I passed out. He did a lot of other horrible things to me.

"In my mind I imagined her hearing this and saying, 'Oh. That's too bad. Well, how long do you think it will take for Felix to fix his computer?' "

No one laughed at my attempt at sick humor. I guess it wasn't really funny.

" 'Are you all right now?' my mother asked. 'Do you need to see a doctor?'

" 'No,' I said. I meant I'm not all right, but she took it to mean I didn't have to see a doctor.

" 'Well, just take it easy. I know you're probably nervous about your appointment with the judge at the end of the month, but it will be fine. That stupid Felix,' she added. 'He's such a . . . what would you say, dork?'

"She waited to see if I appreciated her attempt to speak the lingo. I just stared and she smiled and shook her head and hurried away.

"My father arrived just before dinner. Mother was in the office barking orders at Felix. My father put down his leather case that contained his drawings and listened to her shouting for a moment.

" 'The world of beautiful people appears to be in a crisis,' he declared and laughed.

"There was a time when he would feel sorry for her, sympathize and even offer some suggestions. How far apart they've grown in a few short months, I thought.

" 'And how's my favorite scholar? Did you knock them dead at the induction, make a speech or something?' he wondered.

" 'I didn't go,' I told him. 'I wasn't feeling well.'

" 'Oh, too bad. What was wrong?'

" 'Stomachache,' I said, and he nodded.

" 'Woman stuff?'

"Whenever I had a stomachache or a headache, that was a convenient explanation for him. It was his excuse for not really worrying.

" 'Right,' I said, thinking, why bother?

"He refreshed himself quickly and came to dinner just after my mother finished her phone calls and we began the charade of another family dinner with storm clouds looming above."

"I think I was better off having my father move out," Misty said.

"You're right about that," Star seconded.

"I guess I would agree with both of you now," I said. "Their conversation was clipped, short and shaded with nasty innuendos. Neither really cared to know about the other's day. I suppose neither of them wanted to appear weak by asking a nice question. Before the dinner ended, they managed to get in another argument about me.

" 'She didn't go to the Honor Society induction,' my mother declared just before coffee and dessert.

" 'I heard,' my father said.

" 'I'm sure she was upset about having neither of us attending and that gave her a nervous stomach,' my mother said.

" 'Whose fault is that?' my father countered.

"It was as though I wasn't even there while they argued. Can you understand why I felt I was becoming more and more invisible, a shadow of myself?" I asked the girls. They all nodded.

"My mother wiped her mouth with her napkin and reached into her purse which she had brought to the table and placed on the floor beside her chair. When she had done that, I wondered about it, but I didn't ask. All the while she had anticipated this argument and was preparing for it, I discovered, and so did my father.

"She plucked her appointment book out of her purse and flipped through the pages.

" 'It's very clear that it was your turn to escort Jade to one of her school functions,' she said. 'If you want to check the calendar, it's right here. I went to the P.T.A. function two weeks ago while you were embroiled in a creative meeting in Pasadena. I have it written down. Care to look?' she said, holding out the book.

"My father glanced at me and then turned back to her, furious.

" 'You never mentioned the schedule before the two of us planned our appointments,' he said through his clenched teeth. That's probably where I get doing that. It's one of his precious gifts to me: clenched teeth during anger.

" 'I didn't think I would have to remind you of an obligation to your own daughter,' she returned sharply.

" 'It seems to me you missed something last month,' he said, but weakly because he wasn't nearly as prepared as she was. My mother has always been a lot better than my father at organizational details. He's more creative, abstract, lost in his images and visions. She's more precise, a manager. He was outgunned.

" 'You never mentioned it and I don't recall it, but this is clearly an example of your lack of responsibility when it comes to Jade's needs,' she said, flipping her appointment book closed and dropping it like a dagger back into her purse.

" 'Are you going to run right to the phone and tell your attorney?' he snapped.

" 'It will be properly noted,' she said as Mrs. Caron entered with the coffee and carrot cake.

" 'You just let this happen,' my father continued. Usually, they waited for Mrs. Caron to leave before having any words between them, but he was like a balloon about to burst, his face flushed and his eyes wide and angry. 'It's nothing more than entrapment, plain and simple and disgusting.'

" 'The bottom line is she didn't go to an important school function,' my mother insisted. Her calmness made him angrier. He flustered about a moment and then turned to me.

" 'I'm sorry, Jade, if you didn't go because of me, that is,' he said, hoping I would deny it.

" 'Of course she didn't go because of you,' my mother pounded.

" 'Let her speak for herself. That's something you never let the child do anymore, have her own mind.'

" 'That's ridiculous. I never . . .'

" 'STOP!' I screamed, my hands over my ears. 'I didn't go because I ran away. I flew to San Francisco and I was almost kidnapped and raped and killed and neither of you know a damn thing about it.'

"They both sat there, staring, their mouths open.

" 'What?' my father said. He looked at my mother and she shook her head, her face bright with shock.

" 'I HATE THIS! I HATE THIS!' I shouted, and ran out of the dining room, up the stairs and into my room, slamming the door shut and locking it behind me.

"About ten minutes later, they both came upstairs and stood outside my door together asking me to let them in and explain what I had said. I didn't answer them. My mother went down to question Mrs. Caron, but she knew nothing, of course, except that I had been gone. She couldn't tell how long. I never tell her when I leave, where I'm going or how long I'll be there. How could she be expected to know?

"My father continued to plead with me to tell him what had happened. Finally, they both retreated to their own affairs.

"Later, when I was calm and they asked me again, I told them some of it. Of course, they only blamed each other and threatened to use it against each other in court. My father pushed for more details so he could contact the police, but I didn't want to be part of any of that. Just the thought of seeing Mr. Bennet again sent electric chills through my heart. My parents gave up on it, and around me at least, pretended it had never happened.

"After a while it even diminished in my own mind, probably because as Dr. Marlowe has told me, I am using defense mechanisms to keep from reliving the events. I guess I ruined all that today, huh, Doc?"

"No," she said softly. "Sometimes, the best way to kill your demons is to let them out and expose them to sunlight."

"Like vampires, right, Dr. Marlowe?" Misty said.

Dr. Marlowe laughed.

"Yes, Misty, like vampires."

"What about the crazy man?" Star wanted to know. "Did he ever call you or anything afterward?"

I nodded.

"I couldn't help it," I explained. "In a bizarre way I was drawn back to my computer and sure enough, there was an E-mail from him waiting in my mailbox. Only it was from Craig, not Mr. Bennet, of course."

"What did he say?" Cat asked.

"He apologized for his father's behavior, claiming his father was under a lot of stress these days because he had lost his job and there were financial problems as well as a mountain of emotional ones. He said his little brother Sonny had gotten worse, too, and now he was becoming so withdrawn, he would barely talk to him. The school was recommending psychiatric care and he might have to be institutionalized. I think that was probably what had really happened to him."

"You didn't write back, did you?" Star asked.

"No. I changed my screen name and lost him forever in cyberspace," I said. "Which," I added, "is where I wish I could lose myself these days."

Everyone was absorbed in her own thoughts for a long moment. I took a drink of water and gazed at the clock. When I had first come here in the morning, I thought, I never imagined I would have lasted this long, or have had so much to tell.

"I guess I would have to say the events did sink into my parents' hearts after a while. I know the horrible events changed me and made me withdraw from a lot of things."

I smiled at Dr. Marlowe.

"That's part of why I was sent here," I said. She nodded.

"My grades started to reflect my lack of interest. I dropped out of one extracurricular activity after another. I lost contact with most of my friends. I hated answering questions about my home life and my parents' divorce and how I felt about it. Your life can turn into a soap opera pretty quickly at my school," I said.

Star grunted and nodded. Misty smiled knowingly at Cat who smiled back. She was coming out of her shell more and more, I thought. I guess Dr. Marlowe was right about all this.

"One afternoon when I returned home from school, I was surprised to find my mother already home. She had changed into a pair of jeans and a light blue blouse, put on sneakers and tied her hair with a bright yellow bandanna. She looked younger, younger than I could recall her looking for a long time.

" 'C'mon,' she said as I entered the house and she came out from the kitchen. 'I found this great crystal shop in Santa Monica and I want to get some things for the house. It'll be fun.'

"I was so taken aback, I just stood there with my mouth open, looking stupid. She laughed and urged me to change and come down in five minutes.

"I did and we headed for the beach town. All the way she didn't mention one thing about her job. She said she had been working too hard and been stupid to ignore some of the fun things in life. It was time to reap the benefits of all this hard work, she claimed.

"We had a nice afternoon shopping. She bought me a beautiful crystal to wear around my neck and then we went to a great bakery and picked up some delicious bread and a dozen cookies.

" 'Time to splurge,' she cried. 'Let's not worry about calories tonight.'

"That struck me as funny because she never did and often criticized me for worrying.

"She laughed too, and then she suddenly pulled over on Pacific Coast Highway before heading back to the house so we could look at the ocean. It looked so peaceful with sailboats gliding over glass, their sails floating against the light blue sky.

" 'It's so beautiful here. I often forget and take it for granted,' she said and then she turned to me with as serious and as concerned an expression as I had ever seen.

" 'I don't want you to think I'm totally oblivious to all you've suffered, Jade,' she said. 'And I'm not going to deny my own share of blame. What happened to you recently frightened the hell out of me. I tried to keep from thinking about it, but I couldn't. I'm so lucky you're all right,' she said with tears in her eyes. She fanned her face to stop herself from crying. 'I wouldn't have blamed your father. I would have blamed myself.'

"Then she sucked back her tears and promised things were going to change.

" 'We've got to become more like sisters,' she said. 'I promise I'll set aside more time to be with you. Let's make Saturday lunches our special time together, okay?'

"Of course I agreed, even though in the back of my mind, I could hear my father demanding Sunday lunches for himself or every other Saturday. It was the way things had been.

"But I don't think we ever get tired of hearing our

parents' promises, no matter how many times they break them. It's like buying another lottery ticket after you've lost and lost and lost. You just can't help hoping and fantasizing.

"The following day, my father surprised me by showing up at school at the end of the day to drive me home.

" 'I realized I was nearby,' he claimed, 'and thought it would be nice. How was your day?'

" 'Okay,' I said. It hadn't been. I had failed an important math test and dropped my average so low, it was clear I was going to be kicked out of the Honor Society at the end of the year, but I didn't tell him that.

" 'I know you don't want to talk about your episode in San Francisco anymore, and to tell you the truth, I don't either,' he said with a smile. 'It gives me nightmares, too. It should never have happened and I should never have gone away before the Honor Society induction. I'm sorry,' he said.

"My parents' apologies were like cold raindrops. I hated them and fled from them. I said nothing. I just turned away and gazed out the window.

" 'What it told me was I'm really missing the boat here. I should be enjoying your adolescent years along with you more. I want to be part of what you do and what you enjoy. I've decided to cut back on my workload just for that purpose,' he added. 'Please don't hesitate to ask me to go to anything or be part of anything anymore. Forget schedules. I'll find the time. I'll change dates and meetings.

" 'We should just do more fun things together,' he added. 'Okay?'

"I turned back to him.

" 'Okay,' I said, but now I was so suspicious of both of them, I practically held my breath and kept myself from asking any questions.

"He decided it would be fun to stop to have an old-fashioned ice-cream soda and he knew a place that still made them that way. We drove to the soda shop and he talked about his high school days and told me things he had never told me before about overcoming his own shyness with girls, his first real girlfriend, and his disastrous prom date with someone named Berle Lownstein whose orthodontia retainer fell out while dancing. I couldn't stop laughing at some of it. No matter what his reasons for spending time with me, I thought, I was having a good time. It was fun.

"Suddenly, they were really competing for my attention, my time and filling my days with suggestions of fun things to do. Of course, I hated turning one down because of something the other had already planned, but they didn't argue or fight about it as I expected they would. They seemed to have stepped back to let me have breathing room. I began to suspect they had secretly agreed that they would conduct themselves this way and let the best man win.

"And then it occurred to me one night, that all this had begun after the judge who held the power of granting custody had made the date for my appointment in his office, in camera.

"And I went to sleep full of a new fear. I tossed and turned, shrinking into a tighter and tighter ball.

"What if all their expressions of love and all their fun and warmth was contrived again?

"What if I was still a pawn, a piece on a checker board, an asset, a trophy?

"What if all this was just another battle in their grand war?"

7

"My appointment with the judge was on the following Thursday, at ten in the morning. The limo was taking me there and I had to go by myself so that neither of my parents could influence me. Dr. Morton asked me if I would like her to accompany me and I told her no. I should have said yes.

"I remember how alone I felt in that big backseat. I never really felt so alone in the limo before. It was raining hard. The drops pelted the roof and I thought God must have been angry. They sounded like His bullets. It was so dark and dreary and our travel was funeral procession slow.

"When we arrived at the courthouse, Judge Norton Resnick's assistant Marla greeted me after we pulled to the curb. I had spoken to her on the telephone the day before. She was a tall, slim woman with short blond hair and beautiful blue eyes, the sort of eyes that always accompany a warm smile which radiates through someone's face. Her warmth helped me relax a little, but being in the courthouse where my parents and their attorneys would do battle over possessions, the house and especially me, turned my nerves into thin piano wires on the verge of breaking. As we passed through the metal detectors, my heart skipped. Suddenly, after all these months of talk, talk, talk, everything seemed to be happening so fast. In moments I was being led down a wide corridor with polished marble floors. Voices echoed. Well-dressed men and women passed by us either laughing or arguing. I couldn't help but feel intimidated, out of place and very frightened. My heart was no longer skipping beats. Now it was hammering against my chest.

" 'Right this way, Jade,' Marla said, opening an office door with the judge's name on the front. We entered a small outer office. Marla asked me to wait for a moment and then went through the next door, closing it softly.

"I was afraid to sit, afraid that when it was time to stand again, my legs wouldn't support me. Fortunately, it was only a few seconds later that she emerged and told me to step into the office.

"It was smaller than I had anticipated. Judge Resnick sat behind a sizeable light mahogany desk with large, thick volumes piled on both his right and left and long yellow legal pads in front of him. There were plaques and pictures all over the walls and especially right behind him and beside the American flag. The governor's picture was prominent.

"The judge had two windows that looked out on the street, but raindrops zigzagged like tears, blurring the view.

"Judge Resnick looked to be about fifty, maybe fifty-five, with curly black hair and dark round eyes. He had a thick nose and soft, almost Santa Claus cheeks, each with a light circle of pink at the crest. In his robes he appeared even bigger and heavier than I imagined he was, although when he stood, I saw he was very wide in the waist.

"There was a captain's chair set up directly in front of his desk. On the right, seated at a small table, was the court stenographer. He was a short, thin man with light brown hair, thick glasses, light brown eyes and what I thought was a mouth much too small for his oval face. He barely looked up at me and sat poised, making me even more nervous.

" 'Good morning, Jade,' the judge said with a smile that stretched his thick lips until they were nearly pale. He offered me his stubby fingered hand and I took it for a quick handshake. He nodded at the chair. 'Please, sit,' he said. He nodded at Marla and she quickly turned and left the office.

"I glanced at the stenographer who lifted his hands over the keys of his machine as if he were about to begin a magnificent piano concerto. The judge sat back and pressed his fingertips together. His eyebrows knitted together as he studied me and formed his first impressions.

" 'Let's relax for a few moments,' he began. 'This is Mr. Worth,' he said looking at the court stenographer. Mr. Worth nodded and barely grinned, much less smiled. He didn't seem to ease up a bit, his shoulders and neck remaining stiff. He even looked somewhat impatient.

"The judge cleared his throat.

" 'I don't want you to be nervous about this. I want you to speak freely. I understand from your teachers' reports, your school records, and your counselor that you are a very intelligent young lady. You're not that far away from being on your own, making your own decisions and taking responsibility for your own actions. From what I have seen, you should do very well.' His voice was smooth, easy, relaxed, but I was still on pins and needles.

" 'What we're going to do is have a relatively short conversation about all this so that I can best assess your feelings. I want you to know from the start that for me, you are the most important person in this matter. Your needs must be addressed before anyone else's. I hope you'll be as honest as possible,' he added, 'so I can do the best job for you.'

" 'My grades have slipped recently,' I said. I might as well be as honest as possible right away, I thought.

" 'A huh. And why is that?' he asked, his gaze fixed intently on me.

" 'I guess it's safe to conclude I've been somewhat distracted,' I replied rather dryly. He didn't want to laugh, but I saw a twinkle in his eyes.

" 'Yes, I imagine you have been, and that's part of

what I'd like to learn. What's life been like for you these past few months?'

"I looked away, looked through the wet windows and the haze and the rain. What's life been like? Now there's a question, I thought.

" 'Difficult,' I said. He'd have to press and pry to get me to say much more. You see, right from the start, I was terrified of my answers, terrified of my words," I explained to the others.

"Why?" Misty asked.

"I was afraid I would give an answer that would make him decide in either my mother's favor or my father's and it would be solely my fault. No matter what my complaints have been about them, I didn't want either to hate me, and I didn't want to hurt either.

"Judge Resnick wasn't a bad judge. He must have had lots of experience with cases like mine because he practically read my thoughts, anticipating my fear.

" 'I want you to know,' he said, 'that your comments are very important, but there is testimony from other important people and facts you might not even know yourself. I have other things to consider here.

" 'You're old enough for me to cut right to the heart of this, Jade. Do you have any preference or reason to have preference for one of your parents to have full legal custody of you?'

"How do you answer that if you don't hate one or the other? I wondered. Would a judge ask a parent which child he or she prefers?

"Could I erase all the happy moments I had experienced with either of my parents? Did I have to concentrate on the times I was angry at one or the other so I could harden my heart against my father or against my mother? I wished I could be cut in half or cloned so each would have what he or she wanted.

" 'Do you feel closer in any way with either?' he pursued. 'Or, let me put it this way, do you think one or the other will be more important to you at this stage of your life? I've had girls your age who thought they would need more time with their mothers,' he added, raising those thick eyebrows in anticipation.

" 'I'd like more time with both of them,' I said. He nodded, his eyes encouraging. He just wants me to talk, I thought, to talk and talk and talk.

"So I began. I talked about my parents and their precious careers. I talked about the many times neither had been there for me. I guess I talked about my own loneliness. I laughed at his reference to my soon-to-be-independence. 'Sometimes,' I told him, 'I feel like I've brought myself up. Independence will be no novelty for me.'

"He listened quietly. I got so into it, I stopped noticing the stenographer's fingers taking down my every word with lightning speed. The judge's eyes gradually turned darker. He even looked angry at times.

" 'It's not fair that I'm even here,' I concluded. 'I shouldn't have to do this. It's their problem.'

"When I was finished, he just sat quietly for a moment. His face had become so somber, he looked like a different person. He leaned forward, studied a paper on his desk and then looked up at me and asked, 'What if you lived with neither for the next year? Would that be so upsetting?'

" 'With whom would I live? Where would I live?'

"He began by suggesting one of my grandparents and I laughed aloud then. His eyebrows bounced up and I explained my relationships with my grandparents and how rarely I had spent any time with either my father's or my mother's parents. When he asked about my other relatives, I had the same reply.

"From the way he looked, I imagined I wasn't making it any easier for him. How simple it would be if I would say, 'Oh yes, Judge. I need my mother more now. We have female issues to discuss and my father won't be able to help,' but I had other issues looming before me, and how easy it would be to say I need my father more for them.

"I know what we can do, your honor, I thought, instead of cutting the child in half, cut the parents in half and paste a half of one to a half of the other and give me a new kind of parent, part Daddy, part Mommy, only be sure to cut away the parts full of hate, okay?

"Thinking about that made me laugh and he smiled and asked what struck me funny?

"I decided to tell him and I did. He didn't laugh. He nodded with sadness in his eyes. I glanced at the stenographer whose bland face finally showed some surprise and interest.

"The judge asked me more questions about my

daily routine, my ambitions. He talked about my parents' input into any of it, searching, I was sure, for evidence of one being more concerned than the other. I soon began to feel like a witness being cross-examined by a relentless prosecutor.

"Finally, I told him about my parents' recent expressions of repentance and their new promises about all the time each was going to spend with me and how much fun we would have. He seemed interested until I said, 'But in my house promises are lies tied up with pretty ribbons. Every week our maid vacuums them up and dumps them in the incinerator.'

"I followed that with another nervous little laugh. He asked me if I would like something to drink and I said hemlock. He didn't think that was funny at all."

"What's hemlock?" Star asked.

"Poison. Socrates drank it," I said. Star glanced at Dr. Marlowe and then turned back to me.

"I was tired of all this. The dreariness of the rainy day had moved into my body. I really just wanted to sleep.

" 'So,' Judge Resnick concluded, 'if I turn over legal custody to one or the other of your parents, you won't be that upset about it? Is that a fair assessment?'

" 'Frankly, your honor,' I said, 'I don't give a damn.'

"That's from *Gone With the Wind,* and actually, it was appropriate. *Gone With the Wind* took place during the Civil War and that's what was going on in my house.

"Once again, however, the judge didn't laugh. He scowled, made a note and sat back, very pensive.

" 'Okay,' he said, coming to some conclusion, 'I guess that will be all for now. You've been helpful. I do hope everything works out for you, Jade. You have shown evidence of strength and accomplishment and although I don't want to belittle the significance of all this, I think you're going to rise above it and become a fine young lady.'

"Was he a judge or a fortune teller or was that one and the same? I wanted to ask, but I didn't. I kept silent. Marla was called back in to escort me out to the limousine. I glanced at the stenographer before I left. He looked like he had been bored out of his mind. I guessed it wasn't as exciting as a murder or something.

" 'Judge Resnick is one of the best judges when it comes to these matters,' Marla assured me on the way out. 'He's fair and very wise and he takes a great deal of time and does a lot of research before rendering any decisions.'

" 'Fine,' I told her at the limousine. 'I'll recommend him to all my friends.'

"It wasn't nice to be sarcastic to her, but I was very tired of all of it and she just happened to be a part of it. I did thank her before I got into the car.

" 'Home James,' I said. I've always wanted to say that. The driver glanced at me in the rearview mirror. He was a different driver from the one I had previously had.

" 'My name's not James,' he muttered.

"The rain had slowed to a slight drizzle, but the traffic was just as heavy as before. It was a nauseating ride for me. I closed my eyes to keep my stomach from churning. I hadn't eaten much for breakfast and I was glad of that now.

"I was happy neither of my parents would be home yet. I knew they would each have questions in their eyes and look for some hint as to what I had told the judge.

"Just the thought of that began to weigh heavier and heavier on my mind. I dreaded seeing them at dinner. I dreaded ever seeing them. What was the judge going to do with my testimony? Whose heart had I broken? Why didn't they think about my heart?

"The rain started to come down harder again. It was practically impossible to see out of the windows. The driver grumbled about it, but we continued on. When we reached the house, I just opened the door before he came around and ran inside and shook the water out of my hair.

"It was quiet and dark because Rosina had not turned on the lights in some of the rooms. Mrs. Caron was most likely in the kitchen working on the evening's gourmet meal. No matter what happened here, we would always eat well, I thought, and started up the stairs.

"My body throbbed all over. I didn't realize until that moment just how tense I had been in the judge's office. The back of my neck especially ached. I felt as though I had been in a car accident and now I was experiencing the trauma. This whole thing was like a big crash anyway.

"The urge to just lie down and sleep got stronger and stronger. I undressed and crawled into bed, but whenever I closed my eyes, Judge Resnick's big face appeared and I relived his questions, his expression, his penetrating eyes. Then I began to imagine my mother's disappointed face and my father's. Tossing and turning through these persistent nightmares, I finally sat up, feeling like I could scream and pull the hair out of my head. For a while I just stared at the wall and then I rose, slipped into my robe and went to my mother's room.

"I found her sleeping pills in the nightstand next to her bed and brought them back to my room."

Before I continued, I glanced at Dr. Marlowe and then I glanced at the girls. They all looked like they were holding their breath. I was tempted to smile and say, "That's all," but they all knew it wasn't right and besides, I wanted to tell them. I wanted to get it out, spit it from my body as fast as I would spit out sour milk.

"I thought if I took two pills, I'd be able to get some sleep, and then I thought, if I took three, I'd sleep right through dinner and not have to face them; if I took four, I'd sleep right through the night; if I took five, I'd sleep through breakfast.

"All those thoughts ran through my mind and I guess I started laughing and taking another and another until most of the pills in the bottle were in my stomach. Then I lay back, stared up at the ceiling and waited. My eyelids grew heavier and heavier and finally slammed shut like a steel door.

"It was as if the sleeping pills took me back in time, making me younger and younger until I was just a little girl again, years and years before my parents became the people they were now.

"They were still in love and we were still a family. I saw us doing things together, going to Disney World, going to the beach, going to restaurants. I sat on my father's shoulders when we walked and felt him bouncing me along. I heard my parents' laughter curling around me like a warm, protective cocoon.

"There were lots of kisses then. How safe I felt. Those were the days of my big bubble. It felt so good to return. It was as if all that had happened since was just a nightmare, a long, bad dream. I was waking up and I was calling for them. I could see myself, my mouth opening and closing, but I couldn't hear my voice. Somehow, they must have heard.

"They both came to my room and stood by my bed. They held me tightly and they rained down love and promises. I was drenched in happiness. And then I heard the screams.

" 'Get the paramedics!' Mommy was screaming.

"Why? I wondered. Was there emergency care for nightmares?

"I could hear and sense all the rushing about. Somewhere off to the right, I heard the sound of a siren. And then I heard this heavy, loud drum. It was coming closer and closer and getting louder and louder before I realized it was my own heart.

"Finally, I heard the grating noise of metal screeching as the heavy steel door was being lifted. First, a tiny shaft of light slipped in at the bottom and then the light grew larger and brighter until the door was nearly completely opened.

"As soon as it was, the light diminished and I was able to make out silhouettes behind it. The darkness gradually lifted from their faces and I saw it was my parents looking at me. My mother's mouth was opening and yet I didn't hear her voice. Soon, it became a muffled, far-off sound that slowly got louder and clearer until I understood she was calling my name.

"My father stepped up beside her and did the same. I just stared at them.

"How did they get so much older so fast? I wondered.

"Where am I? I wondered.

"The room was unfamiliar. What happened to my room? Where were all my things? Where was my big bubble?

"I wanted to sleep, but they wouldn't let me. They shook me and called to me until I kept my eyes open.

" 'Where am I, Mommy?' I asked.

"I saw tears on her cheeks. My mother never cried. What was going on? I wondered. I looked at my father. His eyes were glassy, too.

" 'You're in the hospital, Jade, but you're going to be all right,' she said.

" 'That's right, baby,' my father said. 'You're going to be all right.'

" 'Good,' I said. 'Are we going to the beach today?'

" 'Yes,' my father said, laughing, 'we're going to the beach today.'

"My mother smiled through her tears and brushed my hair off my forehead.

"A doctor stepped up beside them and said something too low for me to hear. They nodded and then each kissed me. That's what made me think I was still five years old, I guess. I wanted to hold on to that as long as I could," I added, glancing at Dr. Marlowe again. She nodded.

"My parents turned and walked out of the room and I thought, I could almost swear, they were holding hands. Maybe it was what I hoped I saw," I concluded sadly.

I stared at the floor. After a sigh that was so deep I could feel it in my bones, I looked up.

"It wasn't long afterward that I came to see Dr. Marlowe."

I took a deep breath and looked out the window. No one spoke. We could hear water running through a pipe somewhere off to our right in the house.

"What happened with the judge and all?" Star asked finally.

"It's not completely over," I replied, "but it looks like my parents are going to compromise and agree to joint custody. My father is talking about building himself a new house. He's getting more and more excited about it. He's brought me the plans and showed me where my room would be and he's asked me to make suggestions.

"My mother is talking about a leave of absence

from her job, but I'm not holding my breath. Yesterday, she said the company management was thinking about giving her a significant raise to keep her from leaving, even for a hiatus.

"Things are different in the house. I'll say that. They both seem to tiptoe around me lately and they never argue or even discuss problems when I'm around. In fact, it's just the opposite. They're overly polite to each other. Their war is coming to an end," I said.

"Everyone talks about rebuilding, mending, putting it all behind us. There's a new reality and we've got to learn how to adjust to it," I said, repeating some of the platitudes I had been told.

"I feel like my whole life to this point was written in chalk and a few lawyers, sociologists, yes, even therapists, have come along and helped erase it and start writing new words. Sometimes, I think I should change my name and really go through a rebirth."

"You've got a pretty name," Misty said softly.

I smiled at her. She reached out to touch my hand and hold it for a moment.

"Well," Dr. Marlowe said, "I don't know about you guys, but I think I'm ready to call it a day. You heard Emma before. She practically ordered me to be sure you all enjoyed the nice weather."

I nodded. All the girls were staring at me now. Then Misty smiled and Star quickly followed. Cat joined them and I laughed.

"I guess I talked a lot more than I expected. Sorry."

"No, no, it was fine," Star said.

"Yeah, I'm glad you told us as much as you wanted," Misty said.

Cat nodded.

"Me too," she said in a voice just above a whisper.

We all stood up and Dr. Marlowe led us out of the office and to the front door. My limousine and driver were there already, as was Star's grandmother and Cat's mother. Misty had to call for a cab and we all offered to wait with her.

"No, you don't have to," she said. "It won't be long. I'm used to waiting for cabs these days."

"I bet," Star said and then looked at Cat. "You coming back here tomorrow?"

She looked at each of us, her eyes fearful.

"Yes," she said.

"You'd better," Star said, "or we'll be coming to your house."

"Stop scaring her," Misty ordered. "She'll come. You want to come back, right, Cat?"

Cathy smiled at being called Cat and nodded. She looked toward her mother and lost her smile quickly.

"It's hard," I told her, "but it does help. You'll see." I squeezed her hand.

"Okay, bye," she said in a small voice, and walked to her mother's car. We watched her get in and then drive off. Her mother didn't look our way.

"Granny's scowling at me," Star said. "I better get a move on."

"I guess that's Rodney gaping at us from the backseat," I said.

"That's him," she said with a laugh.

"He looks cute," Misty said.

"Don't let him fool you. Cute only lasts a few minutes every day," she said, and Misty and I laughed. "See you tomorrow, girlfriends," she added and walked quickly to her grandmother's car. "What are you gaping at them like that for?" we heard her yell at Rodney. "They're just girls. Get your head in," she ordered and got into the car.

She smiled and waved to us as they pulled away.

Misty walked with me to the limousine. The driver got out to open the door.

"It is a pretty day. What are you going to do with the rest of it?" she asked.

"I don't know. I have some magazines to read. I guess I'll just lounge by the pool and work on my tan or paint my fingernails. What about you?"

She shrugged.

"Nothing," she said.

"Give me your phone number," I said. "I'll call you later."

"Really?" She gave it to me and I got into the limousine and rolled down the window.

"I guess what happens, what hurts the most," I said, "is you lose faith. You think, if they can fall out of love, the two people you love the most, the two people you idolized and believed in the most, then how can anything beautiful happen between you and someone? Understand?"

"Yes," she said. "Exactly."

I reached out and she took my hand for a moment.

"Maybe, we're better than them," she offered.

"Maybe the best of them is in us and we're even better."

"Maybe," I said.

She let go and stepped back as the limousine started. Her hand had felt like the string on a balloon. As I rode off, the balloon rose in my imagination. Our four faces were on it and we were drifting into the wind.

Drifting toward something better.

Maybe.

POCKET BOOKS PROUDLY PRESENTS

CAT

V.C. Andrews®

The fourth book in the WILDFLOWERS series.

Coming soon in paperback from Pocket Books

The following is a preview of *Cat*. . . .

I woke with a terrible chill. I was shivering even before my eyes had opened. Cringing in bed, I drew my legs up tightly until my knees were against my stomach and I buried my face in the blanket, actually biting down on the soft, down comforter until I could taste the linen. No matter how warm my room was, I had to sleep with a blanket. I had to wrap myself securely or I couldn't sleep. Sometimes, during the night, I would toss it off, but by morning, it was spun around me again as if some invisible spider was trapping me in its web. I could feel the sticky threads on my fingers and feet, and struggle as much as I'd like, I was unable to tear myself free.

Exhausted, I waited, as the spider drew closer and closer until it was over me and I looked up into its face and saw it was Daddy.

Because my daddy went to work so early, my mother was always the one left with the responsibility of waking me, if I didn't rise and shine on my own for school. She would usually do it by making extra noise outside my bedroom door. She rarely knocked and she almost never opened the door. I could probably count on the fingers of one hand how many times my mother had been in my bedroom while I was in it too, especially during the last five years.

Instead, she would wait for me to leave for school, and then she would enter like a hotel maid after the guests had gone and clean and arrange the room to her liking. I was never neat enough to please her, and when I was younger, if I dared to leave an undergarment on a chair or on the top of the dresser, she would complain vehemently and look like the wicked witch in *The Wizard of Oz.*

"Your things are very private and not for the eyes of others," she would scowl, then advance and put her hands on me and shake me as if to wake me. "Do you understand, Cathy? Do you?"

I would nod quickly, but what others? I would wonder. My mother didn't like any of my father's friends or business associates and she had no friends of her own. She prized her solitude. No one came to our house for dinner very often, if at all, and certainly no one visited my room or came upstairs, and even if they had, they wouldn't see anything because Mother insisted I keep my door shut at all times. She taught me that from the moment I was able to do it myself.

Nevertheless, she would be absolutely furious now if I didn't close the Tampax box or not put it back in the bathroom cabinet, and once, when I had left a pair of my panties on the desk chair, she cut them up and spread the pieces over my pillow to make her point.

This morning she was especially loud. I heard her put down the pail on the floor roughly, practically slamming it. She was at her cleaning earlier than usual. The mop hit my door, swept the hard wood floor in the hallway and then hit my door again. I looked at the small clock housed in clear Danish crystal on my night table. The clock was a birthday present from my grandmother, my mother's mother, only weeks before she had passed away from lung cancer at the age of only fifty-one. She was a heavy smoker. My grandfather was twelve years older than she was and died two years later from a heart attack. Like me, my mother had been an only child. Not long ago I found out I wasn't supposed to be, but that's another story, maybe even one that's more horrible than mine. Whatever, one thing was certain: we didn't have much family. Our Thanksgiving turkeys were always small. Mother didn't like leftovers. Daddy muttered that she threw away enough food to feed another family, but he never muttered loud enough for Mother to hear.

Part of the reason for our small Thanksgivings and Christmas holidays was because my father's parents had nothing to do with him or with us, as did neither his sister Agatha nor his younger brother Nigel. My father had told me that no one liked anyone in his family and it was best for all of them to just avoid each other, even each other's funerals. It would be years before I would find out why. It was like finding pieces to a puzzle and putting them together to create an explanation for confusion.

When my mother hit the door with the mop, I knew it was time to rise, but I was stalling. Today was my day at Dr. Marlowe's group therapy session. The other three girls, Misty, Star and Jade, had told their stories and now they wanted to hear mine. I knew they were afraid I wouldn't show up and to them it would be something of a betrayal. They had each been honest to the point of pain and I had listened and heard their most intimate stories. I knew they believed they had earned the right to hear mine, and I wasn't going to disagree with that, but at this very moment, I wasn't sure if they were wrong or right about my appearing.

Mother wasn't very insistent about it. She had been told by other doctors and counselors that it was important for me to be in therapy, but my mother didn't trust doctors. She was forty-six years old and from what I understood, she had not been to a doctor for more than thirty years. She didn't have to go to a doctor to give birth to me. I had been adopted. I didn't learn that until . . . until afterward, but it made sense. It was practically the only thing that did.

My chills finally stopped and I sat up slowly. I had a dark maple dresser with an oval mirror almost directly across from my bed. When I rose in the morning, the first thing I saw was myself. It was always a surprise to see that I had not changed during the night, that my face was still formed the same way (too round and full of baby fat), my eyes were still hazel and my hair was still a dull dark brown. In dreams I had oozed off my bones and dripped into the floor. Only a skeleton remained. I guess that signified my desire to completely disappear. At least that was what Dr. Marlowe suggested at an early session.

I slept in a rather heavy cotton nightgown, even during the summer. Mother wouldn't permit me to own anything flimsy and certainly not anything diaphanous. Daddy tried to buy me some more feminine nighties and even gave me one for a birthday present once, but my mother accidentally ruined it in the washing machine. I cried about it.

"Why," she would ask, "does a woman, especially a young girl or an unmarried woman, have to look attractive to go to sleep? It's not a social event. Pretty things aren't important for that; practical things are, and spending money on frilly, silly garments for sleep is a waste.

"It's also bad for sleep," she insisted, "to stir yourself up with narcissistic thoughts. You shouldn't dwell on your appearance just before you lay down to rest. It fills your head with nasty things," she assured me.

If my daddy heard her say these things, he would laugh and shake his head, but one look from her would send him fleeing to the safety and the silence of his books and newspapers, many of which she didn't approve.

When I was a little girl, I would sit and watch her look through magazines and shake her head and take a black magic marker to advertisements she thought were too suggestive or sexy. She was the stern censor, perusing all print materials, checking television programs, and even going through my schoolbooks to be sure nothing provocative was in them. She once cut illustrations out of my science text. Many times she phoned the school and had angry conversations with my teachers. She wrote letters to the administrators. I was always embarrassed about it, but I never dared say so.

Yawning and stretching as if I were sliding into my body, I finally slipped my feet into my fur-lined leather slippers and went into the bathroom to take a shower. I know I was moving much slower than usual. A part of me didn't want to leave the room, but that was one of the reasons I had been seeing Dr. Marlowe in the first place: my desire to withdraw and become even more of an introvert than I was before . . . before it all happened or, to be more accurate, before it was all revealed. When you can lie to yourself, you can hide behind a mask and go out into the world. You don't feel as naked or as exposed.

I wasn't sure what I would wear today. Since it was my day in the center of the circle, I thought I should look better dressed, although Misty certainly didn't dress up for her day or any day thereafter. Still, I thought I might feel a little better about myself if I did. Unfortunately, my favorite dress was too tight around my shoulders and my breasts. The only reason my mother hadn't taken it out and cut it up for rags was she didn't see me in it for some time. What I chose was a one-piece, dark-brown cotton dress with sort of an empress waist. It was the most recent new dress I had and looked the best on me, even though my mother deliberately had bought it a size too big. Sometimes I think if she could cut a hole in a sheet and drape it over me, she'd be the happiest. I know why and there's nothing I can do about it except have an operation to reduce the size of my breasts, which she finds a constant embarrassment.

"Be careful to step on the sheets of newspaper," Mother warned when I opened my bedroom door to go down to breakfast. "It's still wet."

A path of old newspaper pages led to the top of the stairway where she waited with the pail in one hand, the mop, like a knight's lance, in the other. She turned and descended ahead of me, her small head bobbing on her rather long, stiff neck with every downward step.

The scent of heavy disinfectant rose from the hardwood slats and filled my nostrils, effectively smothering the small appetite I was able to manage. I held my breath and followed her. In the kitchen my bowl for cereal, my glass of orange juice and a plate for a slice of whole wheat toast with her homemade jam was set out. Mother took out the pitcher of milk and brought it to the table. Then she looked at me with those large, round, dark critical eyes, drinking me in from head to foot. I was sure I appeared pale and tired and I wished I could put on a little make-up, especially after seeing how the other girls looked, but I knew Mother would make me wipe it off if I had any. As a general rule, she was against make-up, but she was especially critical of anyone who wore it during the daytime.

She didn't say anything, which meant she approved of my appearance. Silence was yes in my house and there were many times when I welcomed it.

I sat and poured some cereal out of the box, adding in the blueberries and then adding the milk. She watched me drink my juice and dip my spoon into the cereal, mixing it all first. I could feel her hovering like a hawk. Her gaze shifted toward the chair my father used to sit on every morning, throwing daggers from her eyes as if he were still sitting there. He would read his paper, mumble about something, and then sip his coffee. Sometimes, when I looked at him, I found him staring at me with a small smile on his lips. Then he would look at my mother and turn his attention quickly back to the paper like some schoolboy caught peering at someone else's test answers.

"So today's your day?" Mother asked. She knew it was.

"Yes."

"What are you going to tell them?"

"I don't know," I said. I ate mechanically, the cereal feeling like it was getting stuck in my throat.

"You'll be blaming things on me, I suppose," she said. She had said it often.

"No, I won't."

"That's what that doctor would like you to do: put the blame at my feet. It's convenient. It makes their job easier to find a scapegoat."

"She doesn't do that," I said.

"I don't see the value in this, exposing your private problems to strangers. I don't see the value," she said, shaking her head.

"Dr. Marlowe thinks it's good for us to share," I told her.

I knew Mother didn't like Dr. Marlowe, but I also knew she wouldn't have liked any psychotherapist. Mother lived by the adage, *Never air your dirty linen in public.* To Mother, public meant anyone outside of this house. She had had to meet with Dr. Marlowe by herself, too. It was part of the therapy treatment for me and she had hated every minute of it. She complained about the prying questions and even the way Dr. Marlowe looked at her with what Mother said was a very judgmental gaze. Dr. Marlowe was good at keeping her face like a blank slate, so I knew whatever Mother saw in Dr. Marlowe's expression, she put there herself.

Dr. Marlowe had told me that it was only natural for my mother to blame herself or to believe other people blamed her. I did blame her, but I hadn't ever said it and wondered if I ever would.

"Remember, people like to gossip," Mother continued. "You don't give them anything to gossip about, hear, Cathy? You make sure you think about everything before you talk. Once a word is out, it's out. You've got to think of your thoughts as valuable rare birds caged up in here," she said, pointing to her temple. "In the best and safest place of all, your own head. If she tries to make you tell something you don't want to tell, you just get yourself right up out of that chair and call me to come fetch you, hear?"

She paused, and birdlike, craned her long neck to peer at me and see if I was paying full attention. Her hands were on her hips. She had hips that protruded and showed themselves even under her housecoat whenever she pressed her palms into her sides. They looked like two pot handles. She was never a heavy woman, but all of this had made her sick, too, and she had lost weight until her cheeks looked flat and drooped like wet handkerchiefs on her bones.

"Yes, Mother," I said obediently, without looking up at her. When she was like this, I had trouble looking directly at her. She had eyes that could pierce the walls around my most secret thoughts. As her face had thinned, her eyes had become even larger, even more penetrating, seizing on the quickest look of hesitation to spot the lie.

And yet, I thought, she hadn't been able to do that to Daddy. Why not?

"Good," she said, nodding. "Good."

She pursed her lips for a moment and widened her nostrils. All of her features were small. I remember my father once describing her as a woman with the bones of a sparrow, but despite her diminutive size, there was nothing really fragile about her, even now, even in her dark state of mind and troubled demeanor. What it all had done was make her strong and hard like an old raisin, something past its prime, although she didn't look old. There was barely a wrinkle in her face. She often pointed that out to emphasize the beneficial qualities of a good clean life, and why I shouldn't be swayed by other girls in school or things I saw on television and in magazines.

I laughed to myself thinking about Misty's mother's obsession with looking younger, going through plastic surgery, cosmetic creams, herbal treatments. Mother would put nothing more than Ivory soap and warm water on her skin. She never smoked, especially after what had happened to her mother. She never drank beer or wine or whiskey, and she never permitted herself to be in the sun too long.

My father smoked and drank, but never smoked in the house. Nevertheless, she would make a big thing out of the stink in his clothing and hang his suits out on her clothesline in the yard before she would permit them to be put back into the closet. Otherwise, she said, they would contaminate his other garments, and, "Who knows? Maybe the smell of smoke is just as dangerous," she said.

As I ate my breakfast, Mother went about her business, cleaning up after what she had already cleaned up and then she pounced on my emptied orange juice glass, grasping it in her long, bony fingers as if it might just sneak off the table and hide in a corner.

"Go up and brush your teeth," she commanded, "while I finish straightening up after breakfast and we'll get started. Something tells me I shouldn't be bringing you there today, but we'll see," she added. "We'll see."

She ran the water until it was almost too hot to touch and then she rinsed out my cereal bowl. Often, she made me feel like Typhoid Mary, a carrier of endless germs. If she could boil everything I or my father touched, she would.

I went upstairs, brushed my teeth, ran a brush through my hair a few times and then stood there, gazing at myself in the bathroom mirror. Despite what each of the girls had told me and the others about herself, I wondered how I could talk about my life with the same frankness. Up until now, only Dr. Marlowe and the judge and agent from the Child Protection Agency knew any of it.

I could feel the trembling in my calves. It moved up my legs until it invaded my stomach, churned my food and shot up into my heart, making it pound.

"Come on if you're going," I heard Mother shout from below. "I have work to do today."

My breakfast revolted and I had to get to my knees at the toilet, take hold of it, and heave. I tried to do it as quietly as I could so she wouldn't hear. Finally, it stopped and I flushed and washed my face quickly.

She had her light gray tweed short coat on over her housecoat and was standing impatiently at the front door. She wore her black shoes with thick heels and heavy nylon stockings that nearly reached her knees. This morning she decided to tie a light brown scarf around her neck. Her hair was the color of dull silver coins and tied with a thick rubber band in her usual tight knot at the base of her skull.

Despite her stern appearance, my mother had beautiful cerulean blue eyes. Sometimes I thought of them as prisoners because of the way they often caught the light and sparkled even though the rest of her face was glum. They looked like they belonged in a much younger woman's head, a head that craved fun and laughter. These eyes longed to smile. I used to think that it had to have been her eyes that had drawn my father to her, but that was before I learned about her having had inherited a trust when she turned twenty-one.

When my mother accused my father of marrying her for her money, he didn't deny it. Instead he lowered his newspaper and said, "So? It's worth ten times what it was now, isn't it? You should thank me."

Did he deliberately miss the point or was that always the point? I wondered.

I knew we had lots of money. My father was a stockbroker and it was true that he had done wonders with our investments, building a portfolio that cushioned us for a comfortable, worry-free life. Little did I or my mother realize just how important that would be.

The car was in the driveway. My mother had backed it out of the garage very early this morning, washed the windshield and vacuumed the floor and seats. It wasn't a late model car, but because of the way my mother kept it and the little driving she did, it looked nearly new.

"You're pale," she told me. "Maybe you should call in sick."

"I'm all right," I said. I could just hear them all saying, "We knew it. We knew she wouldn't come." Of course, they would be furious about their arriving and wasting time.

"I don't like it," Mother mumbled.

Every time she complained, it stirred the little frogs in my stomach and made them jump against my ribs. I got into the car quickly. She sat at the wheel, staring at the garage door. There was a dent in the corner where my father had backed into it one night with his car after he had had a little too much to drink with some old friends. He never repaired it and every time Mother looked at it, I knew she thought of him. It made the anger in her heart boil and bubble.

"I wonder where he is this fine morning," she said and turned on the engine. "I hope he's in hell."

We backed out of the driveway and started away.